Other Books by Harrison Owen

Spirit: Transformation and Development in Organizations (1987)

Leadership Is (1990)

Riding the Tiger: Doing business in a Transforming World (1991)

Open Space Technology: A User's Guide (1992)

The Millennium Organization (1994)

Tales from Open Space

Harrison Owen
Editor

ABBOTT PUBLISHING
Potomac, Maryland

Copyright ©1995 by Harrison Owen

All rights reserved. No portion of this book may be reproduced by any process or technique without the express written permission of the author.

First published 1995

Printed in the United States of America

ABBOTT PUBLISHING
Post Office Box 56
Cabin John, Maryland 20818-0056
USA

Telephone/Telefax 301-469-9269

Library of Congress Catalog Card Number 95-75969
ISBN 0-9618205-5-1

Introduction

Tales from Open Space is a serious book by serious people. You will find, however, that it is more of a travel log than an academic discourse. There is a good reason. The discovery of Open Space is an ongoing journey, pursued by many people in many lands. The final destination is nowhere in sight and indeed there is every reason to believe that the trip is just barely getting under way. Nobody owns it, nobody can claim full credit for its discovery. Open Space is truly the product of multiple efforts and aspirations.

The journey began, at least as far as my participation, in 1983. That was the year of the First International Symposium on Organization Transformation. Two hundred and fifty people from all over the world gathered to consider the emerging reality of global transformation, and to share what few insights we possessed regarding the successful navigation of the uncharted seas. It was a great meeting as meetings go, but it shared a common failure (or maybe it was a success?) with all other meetings. The formal sessions, although generally outstanding, could not hold a candle to the moments when the real action took place: the coffee breaks.

As a convener of that august gathering, the failure/success was more than disturbing. I had invested an enormous amount of time and effort in the production of the symposium, and discovering that the one thing that everybody liked was the one thing that I had nothing to do with was not pleasing. There had to be a better way.

Two years later, in Monterey, California, eighty-five brave souls showed up for the Third International Symposium on Organization Transformation, and the first experience of Open Space. Without a prepared agenda, knowing only the central theme, and the starting and ending times, this intrepid band created a full three-day agenda. There were multiple workshops, discussion groups, good old get-togethers, all organized in about two-and-one-half hours. There was one facilitator, myself, and I found that my job was to do as little as possible. As a matter of fact, I quickly discovered that the little I proposed to do was greatly in excess of what was required. From the moment of its first manifestation, it was very clear that Open Space bore little if any resemblance to the common experience of the traditional gathering.

For a number of years, Open Space was generally viewed, certainly by myself, as a pleasant but mildly aberrant phenomenon to be enjoyed only at our annual symposia. The thought that it might have general utility in the world of commerce, government, and industry was never seriously entertained. Despite best efforts at nonchalance, Open Space crept into the world of work.

Recently, the passage of Open Space has become something of a rush. It has now been experienced on every continent (with the exception of Antarctica) by groups of 5 to 750. Major government agencies, large international corporations, small community groups, mainline religious bodies, and more have all had the experience of creating intelligent and productive gatherings in a minimum of time with maximum enjoyment. Yes, it is true, Open Space is not only efficient, effective, and productive, but also fun. The original two-and-a-half hours necessary for organization has now been reduced to less than an hour, even with groups of 500. And best of all, my status as solo Open Space practitioner has ended. Presently there are hundreds of people all over the world who regularly demonstrate that Open Space is a global phenomena and definitely not the private magic of Harrison Owen.

What on earth is Open Space? If you are interested in my answer, please consult any or all of my previous books. But a quicker, better way lies at hand. Read on.

In the following material, journalists, practitioners, and participants from around the world share their experience and reflections. I consider them all friends and colleagues, and in the spirit of friendship and collegiality, I have provided a short introduction to each article. There is a loose logic in the sequence, I believe, but please do not expect the whole truth to appear at any one point. By the conclusion, however, I believe you will have a deep appreciation of the rich tapestry which the Open Space experience is quickly becoming. More than anything, I hope you will feel inspired to create a little Open Space yourself.

Table of Contents

Creativity from Chaos
    Don Oldenberg 1

Intense Learning Experience
    Naazneen Karmali 9

Miracles From Open Space
    Srikumar S. Rao 17

Supply and Services Canada
    Paul Tremlett 25

Open Space in a Social Service Setting
    Birgitt Bolton 31

The University of Kentucky Center for Rural Health
    Loyd Kepferle and Karen Main 39

Women's Ways of Leading
    Elaine Cornick and Patricia Montgomery 45

Open Space for the Men's Movement
    Dick Gilkenson 53

"Eur-Open Space"
　　Christopher Schoch 63

Open Space: An Organization Transition Methodology
　　Hugh Huntington 83

Lessons from Open Space at the World Bank
　　Giles and Robbins Hopkins 97

Opening Small Spaces
　　Larry Peterson 113

A Letter from South Africa
　　Barry Lessing 121

Eur-Open Space II
　　Roger Benson 125

Open Space in the Antioch Management Program
　　Jan Gray 131

Safe Space
　　Suzanne Maxwell 149

Chapter I

Creativity from Chaos

Don Oldenburg

Don Oldenburg was the first writer in a major US publication to recognize the potential of Open Space. His article, which appeared in the Washington Post *(February 20, 1992), neatly caught the sense of difference and surprise that typically greets the appearance of Open Space. One might argue with his fixation on chaos as a major theme, for in fact Open Space events exhibit high levels of complex structure and orderly purpose sometimes painfully absent in other meeting formats. However, viewed from the vantage point of the conventional meeting management wisdom, chaos is not only likely, but a predictable result of the Open Space approach. At a deeper level, Oldenburg's reference to chaos is right on the money. From chaos theory we are learning that chaos has an order, and indeed, that chaos is an essential ingredient to the creative process.*

No one's in charge. There is no structure, no agenda, no planned content. Posted on the wall are two hand-drawn signs. One reads simply, "The Law of Two Feet," and shows a crude rendition of two footprints. The other lists four principles that clarify nothing: "Whoever comes is the right people"; "Whatever happens is the only thing that could have"; "Whenever it starts is the right time"; and "When it's over it's over." Whether or not what happened in Ballroom C at the Sheraton Crystal City one morning two weeks ago was the only thing that could have happened is debatable. That it was the strangest conference 50 senior administrators of the U.S. Forest Service have ever attended, no one is debating.

"The most puckered, tight, hierarchy in Washington" is how one of the Forest Service participants described the gathered bureaucrats as they mulled about, sipping coffee, re-checking watches, waiting for "the meeting" to begin. They seated themselves in folding chairs arranged in a large circle. With their arms crossing their chests in classic defensive posture, they looked at the ceiling, looked at each other. All they knew was they were scheduled to be there all day.

"You never know what's going to happen," Harrison Owen says as an aside before he steps to the center of the circled administrators to get things started. Unlike most experts in organizational behavior, Owen thrives on ambiguity and believes that, in the right circumstances, workplaces do too. His theories fly in the face of business as usual. While others try to boost productivity by reorganizing and controlling, he dabbles in chaos, promoting it as a potent creative force. Others focus on the nitty-gritty of organization; he tunes in to the spirit.

Calling his work "organizational transformation," Owen has applied his innovations at major corporations on five continents, as well as with small tribal villages in West Africa, personnel managers in India, and polymer chemists at DuPont. No matter the audience, skepticism always greets his offbeat approach. He expected nothing less from the forestry managers toward the largely leaderless and formless meeting he calls Open Space Technology.

"Every single group I have ever worked with has told me up front it's a great idea but it will never work with them," says Owen, president of H.H. Owen and Co., his consulting firm in Potomac. "Groups that I think I could never get them to do it, like the senior executives for Pepsi-Cola in Venezuela, they take to it like ducks to water."

Were it not for the savvy corporate execs and hard-core senior managers who attest to the effectiveness of Open Space Technology, it might seem like Harrison Owen has hit upon a fat scam in the business world grasping desperately for new solutions. By his own estimate, he spends only about five minutes preparing for these one to five-day conferences. His corporate rate runs about $2,000 a day (though he donated his services to African villages and other promising causes). He readily admits that once he gets a group moving in the right direction, he "goes and sits down the hall." For the Open Space experience to work, he says, no one can take charge – including himself.

"That's the big secret," says Owen, whose credentials include Anglican priest and author of several management books. "I don't do anything. There's nothing to plan – just when is it going to be, and where, and who's coming. My major job is to get them to stop doing things. I have to tell them, 'Don't worry, it's going to happen.' "

What does happen isn't predictable, nor is it easily defined. In a sense, Open Space Technology is kind of the brainstorming version of the classic "Stone Soup" story: Owen's minimal guidance is like the rock in a pot of boiling water, everyone else contributes their ideas to the soup, and in the end the group is well-fed.

"It's like community Rorschach," says Owen, referring to the highly interpretable ink-blot psychology test that is impossible to fail so long as one participates. "The structure that will emerge, will emerge as a response. My goal is that within an hour, we will have the whole agenda for the entire conference and the people to carry it out."

For the first 15 minutes, the Forest Service managers listen soberly to Owen's briefing. He assures them Open Space Technology has worked before, often, and sometimes brilliantly. There was the time the National Education Association brought 420 teachers, school board members and administrators to Colorado to explore how to enhance education in America; in less than an hour they created 85 workshops and then ran the two-day conference themselves.

Last fall, the Forest Service's own travel-and-management division hosted 224 people representing 65 organizations – from the Sierra Club to timber companies to the National Nude Sunbathing Society – to meet on the issue of access to public land. In less than an hour, they created 62 task forces and managed the conference themselves for two days. "About the only thing they had in common was the issue at hand and their antagonism for each other," says Owen. "But by the end of the second day, we had available a 200-page report of their findings. The only complaint was the report was too detailed to assimilate."

If Owen has reinvented the meeting, he's done it by recognizing that creativity abhors a vacuum. His instructions to the forestry mangers are brief: Each is to think of an area or issue he or she is passionate about that relates to the conference's theme ("Enhancing Relationships With Our Customers"); then title it, be prepared to take responsibility for it, step forward and write the title on a piece of poster paper, and tack it to the wall.

The room buzzes with doubt and excitement. "Think of something which is important to you," encourages Owen. "And if nothing pops up, don't worry about it."

One man rises reluctantly, states his name and issue and starts writing it on poster paper. Two more stand up, followed by a flurry of others. Squeaking felt-tip markers compete with voices announcing topics: "Consumption and Recycling," "Whistleblowers: How Can We Be Known Again as an Honest Agency?" and "Multiculturalism."

As sudden as it started, it stops. Buying time for late-blooming ideas, Owen "orchestrates the flow" of what will occur for the rest of the day: The posted topics are arranged in immediate, late morning, and afternoon time slots and are designated locations. Anyone interested in an issue signs up and shows up. Those who originate the issue take notes of what goes on.

Thirty-two minutes into the conference, the forestry mangers have created and scheduled 13 workshops. Owen sends them off, telling them only to report back later that afternoon.

"People say how do you get substantive results out of that?" Owen says afterward. "But the same people who would be sure there was no way anything useful could get done all of a sudden find themselves operating with absolutely no problems in a situation where leadership is constantly changing and structure is made and remade to fit the task at hand. Suddenly the barriers go down."

Owen's credo is "Structure Happens." As he told the Forest Service managers, "What we're really talking about is inspired performance. Can you force inspired performance? You can evoke it. You can give space for it. You can train for it . You can hope for it. You can pray for it. But can you force it? No."

Looking over the workshop choices, Paige Ballard says he's never been to a meeting like this. "It sure seems to encourage creativity and free thought," says the Forest Service's recycling program manager. "It isn't inhibiting about what we can talk about and who can talk about it. And everybody gravitates to what they're comfortable with. Different strokes for different folks."

Bill Delaney, the Forest Service's branch chief for management improvement who has contracted with Owen for several such conferences with other Forest Service departments, believes Open Space works especially well for the silent majority – most of the people in a bureaucracy who usually say the least. "It's not for every meeting," he says, "but it is certainly a way to get participative juices flowing."

Owen designed Open Space Technology seven years ago after a meeting with a group of organizational experts in Monterey, Calif. At the end, everyone confessed they got more out of the coffee breaks than the meeting itself. "So my question was, 'Is there a way of producing the kind of good, intense interaction you get in a coffee break while achieving the output and performance you get in a meeting?'" he says.

"I was looking for a mechanism that was so simple that you could do it in a board room or in a Third-World village with the same results. When all is said and done, people really have the experience of open power. They are in charge – which is the reason the level of spirit and creativity are so high."

Last spring, in South Africa, Owen conducted a one-day Open Space meeting that included the mayor of Cape Town and several black leaders. "I'll never forget. We were all standing in this circle at the end and everybody was crying," says Owen. "They were saying that they were the new South Africa and there was a lot of work to do.

"Open Space seems to create an incredible sense of community. The key is, it's a safe space within which people can take authority and responsibility for themselves." (©*1992 The Washington Post. Reprinted with permission)*

Chapter II

Intense Learning Experience

Naazneen Karmali

Open Space Ttechnology was born and developed in the interesting but protected environment of the several International Symposia on Organization Transformation. It would be fair to state that initially nobody took it very seriously; the rather remarkable results achieved in terms of speed of organization, intensity of conversation, and creativity of output remained unnoticed, or else were attributed to the special quality and characteristics of the symposium participants. Certainly one would not anticipate similar results with a "normal group" in a more standard meeting/conference environment. However, when it was determined in 1988 that an international conference on learning in organizations would be useful, the complexities of multi-national conferencing gave us no choice. The luxury of careful advance planning was simply not available. Open Space Technology appeared as the best option, and from some points of view, the only option. Imagine our surprise when we discovered that it worked. Nazneen Karmali, now managing editor of Business India, *was a participant, and what follows is her report.*

For those who subscribe to the limited view that the sole purpose of business is to generate profits, the concept of business as a process for learning would appear an alien one. That precisely was the theme of the five-day working conference organized by the Taj Continuing Education Programs earlier this month. The setting – a palm-fringed beach resort in Goa – was perfect for exploring this seemingly abstract idea that has caught the attention for human resource development (HRD) managers and management consultants worldwide.

The idea of this conference germinated in November last year when V.S. Mahesh, vice-president (human resources), Taj group met American management guru Harrison Owen, at another conference in Mexico. "We discovered," explains Mahesh, "that of the many concerns of a CEO, the prime one for the nineties is the problem of lifelong learning." Accordingly, the two got together and decided to have a working conference which would endeavor to deal with this idea.

Owen, an Episcopal priest by training, has been a consultant specializing in organizational transformation and development for the last 10 years. For him, the conference theme seemed a logical extension of a paper he had earlier written – "The business of business is learning." According to him, "the global forces of change make it an absolute demand that businesses should adopt a learning mode."

This means, in effect, that learning should become the core activity around which everything else within the organization revolves. While this may appear to be an esoteric exercise, it does hold the promise of concrete benefits: lower manpower turnover, high staff morale, a collaborative and healthy union-management equation and better productivity, profitability and growth.

The 30-odd participants were handpicked – participation being by invitation only – and mainly from the personnel management field. Practising managers in Indian companies, teachers, consultants and management writers from both India and abroad, together formed a formidable bank of knowledge and experience.

Invitees arrived with varying levels of expectation. Rajesh Vidyasagar, general manager, personnel, VST Industries Ltd, Hyderabad, came "to meet creative people from creative organizations and learn from them". The venerable Dr. K.S.Basu, founder-director of the Jamnalal Bajaj Institute of Management Studies, Bombay, approached it with some degree for skepticism. Jagdish Parikh managing director, Lee and Muirhead, being a businessman and the sole representative for the CEO community was curious to see how his views would coincide with those of the others.

Multicultural Mix

Of the foreign visitors, Ronnie Lessem, author and management teacher at London's City University Business School, who was on his first visit to India, had a clear objective: to share western management perceptions and pick up eastern principles. For Anne Stadler, a TV producer with King TV in Seattle, who had made documentaries on India in the past, it was being back in familiar territory. The conference theme tied in with her interest in organisational transformation. This multicultural mix was to throw up an interesting crossflow of ideas emanating from totally different mind-sets and experiences.

Apart from its novel, forward looking theme, another unique facet of the conference was the technology employed. The facility of on-line networking by computer made the conference a truly electronic one. Developed by the Virginia based Meta System Design Inc, the Meta network enabled, in theory, each participant to log in and communicate via the host computer in Virginia with their American counterparts. Sadly though, the telephone lines in Goa refused to co-operate and the marvels of the technology at hand remained a mystery for most participants.

But by far, the most unique characteristic of the conference was the manner in which it was conducted. No advance agendas were set of keynote addresses prepared or papers expected to be presented. Owen, as chief orchestrator, opted for an approach which he calls "open space technology" which gives people the option of creating their own time and space. In most conferences, Owen explains, people say it is the coffee breaks that are the most enjoyable part. Therefore, he decided, creating an environment of coffee breaks would evoke more response and involvement.

How exactly does "open space" work? The circular seating arrangement sans tables, provides a clue. After an initial round of introductions, Owen went on to explain that the agenda and structure would have to be created by the participants themselves keeping in mind the four guiding principles:

➢ Whoever comes is the right person.
➢ Whatever happens is the only thing that could have.
➢ Whenever it happens is the right time.
➢ When its over, its over.

Accordingly, the agenda evolved on the basis of the simple and informal practices followed in the village market place and the scout camp. Any participant who cared to share or explore a particular idea or concept simply wrote it out in brief on a paper sheet which was tacked onto the wall. Those wishing to join a certain discussion group had only to sign up for it. The time and venue for the discussion were set by mutual convenience. People were free to join or break off from any group and set their own pace of participation. The only musts were two meetings at 9 am and 5:30 pm everyday to take stock of the day's proceedings. The summary of each group discussion had to be logged into the computers located in the common conference room.

There was minor pandemonium as the group splintered into four separate, sub-groups. The topics of discussion ranged from the metaphysical – "achieving self-actualisation through work" – to the practical – "how to renew an old and dying organization". A bold but none the less complex question, "What is learning?" formed a part for one set of deliberations. Another pertinent issue raised was that of "resolving the conflict between teamwork and interpersonal competition". These discussions took place over the next three days – the final day being devoted to the summary.

The deliberations of day one were confined to the conceptual. The intellectual process was put on display as participants presented a series of alternative models and flow charts. Debates were heated but there was a certain element missing. It soon became evident that merely cerebral thinking would not do. Prasad Kaipa, employed with Apple Computer Inc, admitted in dejected tones, "I don't feel I have learnt anything".

This not only echoed the feelings of the group, but also precipitated a subtle transformation which took place in the discussions of the following day.

As Owen reports, "It seemed as if we had entered on a common journey in which our collective and individual consciousness was both the vehicle and the object of inquiry". Defenses were totally let down and group members shared experiences freely and openly. This flow was kept up until the final day. And the richness of thought and ideas that were generated was evident from some of the findings.

Vision Statement

Out of one group emerged a vision statement for the organisation of the nineties and the specific strategic actions that business leaders should take. The central feature of an evolved organization would be permitting ordinary people to actively participate in core activities. The business leader should, it was felt, play the role of an enabler and facilitator by providing a supportive environment, an atmosphere that is secure and friendly.

A set of nine action plans were chalked out to make business leaders learning community developers. An important plan that emerged was the need to develop global learning centres for transformational management. The human resource manager would, necessarily, have a key role to play in any learning system. Indeed the onus would be on him to make it happen.

The complex task of defining learning was taken up by another group. Here, a distinction was made between conceptual knowledge and that gained through experience. Quite often learning is associated with pain or even a sense of emptiness. Anxiety tends to create blocks to learning and recall. Different kinds of learning modes and styles were discussed as well as how they could be integrated into executive development programmes both in the US and India.

Intense debate was the hallmark of the group discussion on teamwork versus interpersonal competition. Do people in pursuit of individual recognition give their whole-hearted contribution to the team's goals? Both views, negative and positive, were expressed. But significantly, the conclusion was that if people could be charged with a sense of purpose, then each team member would strive to excel, at the same time, contributing considerably to the team.

This conclusion was arrived at by drawing on the example of the conference itself. Though individuals were given open space, each one got deeply involved and gave his/her best. Therefore, much better results could be obtained by creating such spaces within organisations. The feasibility of the concept was argued, but the consensus was that by demonstration and example – even though it may be in the face of substantial opposition – an effort could be made.

Flood of Ideas

There was veritable outpouring of ideas and the above represent just some of them. Owen terms this, "an explosion of the spirit". Lessem says he was struck by the variety and calibre of the thinking: "There was a marvelous give and take." For Anil Sachdev, general manager personnel, Eicher Motor Ltd, New Delhi, the conference broadened his global perspective of business. A deep sense of achievement, of having arrived at an important conclusion in their work lives, was felt by all.

The conference in Goa, termed the Fort Aguada Beach Resort, India Conference (FABRIC), will be followed by its counterpart a month later in the hills of West Virginia, USA. The output of both these conferences will eventually be compiled in the form of a book to be published in January next year.

As Owen sums up: "We started on a quest. And it turned out to be a remarkable journey into a collective consciousness". In that, the conference was a truly intense learning experience.

(© 1989 Business India *Reprinted with permission*.)

Chapter III

Miracles From Open Space

Srikumar S. Rao

Srikumar Rao is a professor of marketing who, in addition to his academic duties, consults and writes in the area of innovative management approaches. His material appears in many places, including Success, *where a slightly edited version of this present article may be found (November 1992). Although he is an academic, his knowledge of Open Space comes from direct experience and personal application: he uses it with his department and his clients. Sometimes given to hyperbole – forgivable possibly on the grounds that, after all, he is in marketing – Srikumar's interest in the bottom line comes through loud and clear, providing a grounded and very useful insight to the world of Open Space. After all, if Open Space does not contrtibute at the point where the rubber meets the road, its long-term utility is open to question.*

The U.S. Forest Service manages more land than the state of Texas. The largest recreation provider in the country, more than 30 million persons troop through its preserves each year. Its more than 45,000 employees range from forest officers to scientists studying global warming. It is a button-down, strait-laced agency, very conscious of status and protocol. Not a place where you would expect radical change to rear its head.

Several years ago Bill Delaney, branch chief for management improvement, sent a letter to the entire Forest Service asking for people at all levels and all jobs who were interested in talking about how to "Raise the Spirit of the Forest Service." In response, 310 persons gathered in a conference center in Minneapolis. They ranged from F. Dale Robertson, Forest Service Chief, to garage mechanics and included roughly half the top executives of the agency. There was no announced agenda. The air of mystery unnerved managers who mulled around, looked at each other, and waited for the "presentations" to start. Consultant Harrison Owen arranged them in a circle, stepped into the center, and introduced them to a new method of organizing conferences that he calls "Open Space Technology." In 38 minutes flat the vitalized group self-organized a 3-day meeting. Members created and ran 32 different workshops which gave birth to a large package of proceedings, all with no advance preparation. By the end of the third day a new sense of community was palpable. Spirit had descended on the group as it has on all those who have ventured into Open Space.

Barely 3 years after Owen invented "Open Space Technology" and pioneered its use, the technique is raging through the world with the abandon of a computer virus. The French corporation ACCOR, the largest hotel chain in the world, uses it to evolve a vision for the company and formulate business strategy. Owens Corning has used it to develop new products. DuPont has used it to reposition a dying product category. Township leaders in South Africa are using it to shape an ideal of the emerging country. It is being used in India and Venezuela, by giant multinationals and tiny entrepreneurial ventures, by international organizations such as the World Bank and domestic agencies like the National Education Association; and, every time it is used, it leaves converts in its wake.

Group after skeptical group has tried the technique and been wonderstruck by the unexpectedly bountiful harvest. Albany Ladder, a $25 million regional distributor of construction equipment, is so delighted with Open Space that it uses it regularly for its annual planning meeting. Forty-five to fifty employees, constituting top management, middle management, and rank-and-file, sneak away for 3 days and nights each year. Participation is heated, with a dozen or more breakout sessions taking place simultaneously. There are no meal breaks – members grab food on the run as and when they feel like.

When asked if Open Space events have produced any substantive results, Jim Ullery, vice president and director of training, scratches his head in puzzlement. There have been so many that he doesn't quite know where to begin.

There was the time when a breakout group conceived a new line of scaffolding, merged it with a training program and a safety program, and presented it as a brand new product offering. Engineers passed on the blueprints within 2 months and the product was on the market within 6. Total investment was over $3 million and the product is doing very well, thank you. "In the old days it would have taken over 18 months and cost God knows what," says Ullery with a chuckle.

There was the time another group dreamed up a teleprospecting program to open up nontraditional markets for a high-priced personnel lift. Inside of 2 months, 80 demonstrations had been set up. Six months later five products have been delivered, eight orders are being processed, and several others are expected shortly. The company is busy setting up a full department to handle the business. As an aside, the program has been so successful that the manufacturer of the item is making plans to take it to all its distributors nationally.

There was the time when a group decided that a department reported to the wrong person and redrew the organization chart. Neither the existing nor the new supervisor was present in the group. The new arrangement has proven itself much more efficient and nobody can quite figure out why they didn't do it that way to begin with. There was the time...

In an industry plagued by recession and stalked by bankruptcy, Albany Ladder has achieved an average growth rate of 20% over the last 5 years. Ullery lays the credit for this squarely on the esprit de corps engendered by the company's elaborate training programs, many of which include a healthy dose of Open Space. War stories abound of how spirited and empowered employees have spontaneously gone the extra mile to service customers who then come back again, and again, and again.

Open Space conferences are unpredictable and can be initially unsettling. In Minneapolis, managers of the Forest Service were skeptical about the value of a meeting with no agenda, and nervous about a format that permitted the lowest level employee to actually initiate and preside over a session. That very openness created a ferment. Issues bubbled up that would normally never have surfaced, and certainly never have been discussed. Racism, sexism, barriers to advancement, methods of empowering people...all topics were fair game. Individual and group dialogue occurred at such a gut level that many participants broke down. A senior executive with over 30 years of service declared that it was the most powerful meeting he had been to in his entire career. Many lower-level employees reported feeling, for the first time ever, a valued part of the Service. It was precisely this level of openness and communication that Dale Robertson had hoped to foster.

That communication did not end in Minneapolis. Many participants tried to replicate the conference in the home organizations they returned to. They kept in touch with their group members and started introducing big and small changes. "These changes cover the whole gamut of Forest Service management," reports Delaney. One group, for instance, thought that there should be more opportunities for Forest Service employees to trade jobs in career-enhancing ways. This would permit, for example, a Vermont forest officer to experience the Arizona desert. The group put together a proposal and ironed out the wrinkles, and the Job Swap program was eventually approved by headquarters in Washington and put in place. Never before, in the history of the Forest Service, had such an initiative been undertaken and completed by lowly district-level personnel.

Open Space Technology works across culture, nationality, and language. Juan Lopez, a California consultant who has used the method extensively with Hispanic businesses and not-for-profit organizations, reports equally startling outcomes. Longstanding conflicts are resolved, company visions formulated, and a deep,

deep camaraderie established. "If I hadn't seen it countless times, I would never have believed it," he says, shaking his head. What astonishes him most of all is that while creative solutions are being devised for serious problems there is also a light-hearted gaiety in the air. The participants are actually having *fun*. "High Learning" is present, but so is "High Play" and they complement each other marvelously.

When married to modern electronic communications, the results can be even more spectacular. Participants at different locations – even in different continents – can access the results of work group discussions, send or receive "real-time" messages, and tap into a central, continuously updated, database. Lisa Kimball, CEO of Metasystems Design Group, Inc., has set up computer conferencing systems for many Open Space events. "The one slight problem with Open Space," she says, "is that you develop this incredible rapport with your fellows. And then the group breaks up and the rapport gradually dissolves." Computer conferencing and database maintenance solve this problem. "You can call-up the results of discussions you had," continues Carlson, "You can relive your experience. You can send email messages to any or all of your group members and hear back from them instantly. With such easy communication the fervor remains high for months and months. You never lose the rapport that you develop." Carlson firmly believes that it is just a matter of time before Open Space conferences are held which simultaneously involve thousands of persons at many different locations in the world. "You need to be able to do that," nods Owen, "If you are discussing important topics such as global unity and world ecology."

There is little doubt that Open Space Technology will continue to be used widely with businesses leading the way. Revitalized and playful employees will devise powerful new products and more efficient processes. However, it remains to be seen if it will help foster Global Unity or generate consensus on environmental issues. The jury is still out...but strange things happen regularly in Open Space.

For further information:
Srikumar S. Rao
25 Shirley Court
Commack, New York 11725
USA
Telehone 516-864-3146
Fax 516-864-3143

Chapter IV

Supply and Services Canada

Paul Tremlett

Paul Tremlett and his wife, Donna Nelham, are Toronto-based consultants with a practice focused in large part on the federal government. For several years they had been working with a particular client, and more recently had suggested Open Space as a useful approach for the annual departmental gathering. The initial response was interested, but hardly overwhelmed. After all, these strange things born and bred south of the border were always creeping north, and one had to be especially careful. Besides, entering into a large meeting without extended, detailed, and painful planning was obviously risky and probably un-Canadian. But it happened.

Supply and Services Canada is a federal government department with approximately 7500 employees. It is the government's purchasing agent and does virtually all the buying for every department. It also provides a variety of centralized services for other departments, most notable of which is its role as Receiver General for Canada. Its mandate here is to take in all monies paid to the federal coffers and issue all payments to citizens (e.g., tax refunds, pension cheques) and to suppliers of goods and services. It has been, like most organizations today, undergoing significant change for several years and it faces even more in the months and years ahead. It has invested heavily in new technology, it has been downsizing, and there have been changes in its "common service" role.

Each year, the "executive level" managers of the department gather for 2 days to confer essentially about the direction of the organization. This has historically been a time for the most senior managers (the deputy minister and the assistant deputy ministers) to communicate their plans for the organization in the coming year and beyond and to receive ideas and feedback from the approximately 150 key managers in the department. Reportedly, communication at the conferences was mostly one way and there was little real dialogue or true planning done.

A new deputy minister was appointed this year, a client of our firm from two of her previous assignments. My partner, Donna Nelham, and I had, on more than one occasion, discussed the concept and process of Open Space with her. When her staff (some in administrative roles, others in support roles) responsible for planning and running the executive conference were searching for "a new and innovative" way to carry it off (due to growing dissatisfaction with it by all involved), she offered up the idea of Open Space Technology. Her folks were mostly intrigued by the idea, yet hesitant. To their credit, however, they pursued the proposal with open minds, convincing themselves and the senior executive committee that what they needed to do was stop talking about it and "just do it."

I was hired to assist both in the (minimal) preparations involved as well as to lead the process during the conference itself. Due to the need for bilingual (French language) capability, I reached out to a colleague, Bruna Nota, to assist me. Bruna was not familiar with the Open Space concept but is an incredibly quick learner and one whose values and beliefs are congruent with those of Open Space. The department's decision to go ahead was very close to the event itself so it did not give us much time to get ready. I had not worked with such a large group before and would like to recognize Larry Petersen of Toronto who kindly gave us some great counsel and good "logistics" ideas to run with. The conference began with an opening session of about 50 minutes, in which members of the senior executive committee held a brief "public" meeting to share, in dialogue format, the content of the strategic thinking they had been engaged in with the new deputy and to pose the theme for the conference, namely, "A Leader For Administrative Excellence In Government." Following a brief break, we launched the community into Open Space.

Some key highlights about this Open Space event are:

➤ Considerably less time and money was spent in planning and preparation compared to previous years. Instead of sending each participant a 4 inch thick briefing binder in advance of the conference, each received a 10 page document outlining the strategic initiatives the senior executives had been discussing and which set the context for the conference theme.

➤ The 160 managers in attendance developed and posted 47 session topics in 14 minutes. The group took only 50 minutes to structure itself into 29 sessions stretching over a day and a half.

➤ Various forms of session-recording options were available, including laptops, and a central support group was available to publish as things went along (a very different, and less stressful, role for the conference organizing staff).

➤ A powerful, and fun, closing session occurred.

➤ The conference produced a slim, but meaningful, 57-page record of proceedings which included the plans and committments generated by various groups and individuals.

➤ An electronic assessment survey was experimented with which included several questions about the process, all of which were most favorable.

One anecdotal highlight for me was a conversation with one of the participants who pointed out one of his colleagues and said, "You see Tom over there. He's been coming to these meetings, like me, for about 10 years. In all that time, he has virtually not said a word at any of the conferences. This year he's leading a working session. This process is really something to have that happen!"

Some learning Bruna and I experienced:

➤ Several of the women participants indicated their understanding that women were not welcome at the meetings held in the Agora (market place) of ancient Greece. It was a "men only" affair. If this feedback is valid historically, we need to be careful not to overly extol the concept of the Agora.

➤ Stating the one law as the "law of two feet" can have potentially damaging effects on any participants who are disabled (i.e. in wheel chairs, etc.). Also, the expression does not translate into French very well. We changed the law to the "law of mobility" (*mobilité*) which appeared to solve both "problems."

For further information:
Paul Tremlett /Donna Nelham
The Corhe Group
615 Mt. Pleasant Rd./Ste 323
Toronto, Ontario M4S 3C5
CANADA
Telephone 416-440-0044

Chapter V

Open Space in a Social Service Setting
(Keeping the Spirit Alive)

Birgitt Bolton

Birgitt lives on the edge. Why she chooses to do so is a mystery, but nonetheless that is where she chooses to live. Her work at the Wesley Urban Ministries in Hamilton, Ontario, is nothing short of inspiring, as she and her colleagues provide the slim, but critical, difference between making it marginally and going under for many of the lost and forgotten in the Steel City of Canada. With little if anything to take the sharpe edge off a far from pleasant reality, Open Space has become an essential part of their organizational life. No longer a luxury, it appears as a much needed lift to the Spirit of the place.

I have been doing considerable thinking about the everyday use of Open Space Technology as a means of keeping Spirit alive. Of course, one is constrained by "the givens" of organizational life, the things that *have to be* in place, but that leaves lots of room for other uses of Open Space.

When we use Open Space Technology within our regular business, for example staff meetings, there are always comments about that being the best part, and there is always a new burst of energy/life/Spirit. Within the time-frame of a meeting, time for Open Space is reduced, but the results are the same and consistent.

To have Spirit alive and well is an amazing phenomenon in an organization, such as my own that is chronically underfunded; has minimal staff in relation to the workload, terrible hours, and low wages; is the bottom end of the social safety net in our community; and exists in a time of serious recession/depression. Every individual who works within our organization has the Spirit and capacity for leadership (as they do in other organizations). But with us it perculates everywhere. Incidentally, this makes my own senior staff position almost unnecessary, while at the same time it challenges me at my own outer limits as I've never been challenged before.

Long-term effects from Open Space may be limited by defensive personality types, normal behavior for blocking change (because of an individual's fears or desires), the dynamism/operating style/analytical ability of the senior staff persons, and continuing support for the senior staff person in maintaining the energy necessary to be the enabler or holder of time/space for the organization. All of these factors are not as critical in a limited Open Space event as they become in the ongoing work life of an organization.

Now, I'm not saying that lasting change hasn't happened in short-term uses of Open Space because, in fact, people do come away knowing that a different way is possible. I'm even sure that the natural organization which organically emerges in the course of an Open Space event can continue in some way, if only minimally, for many months. But, what then? I think the *what then* can be a continuation of what began in the Open Space event. But that does not just happen ☐ it takes work and ongoing support.

Growing Open Space

At my place of work, chaos is embraced, change is an everyday part of life to be celebrated. We are always positioning ourselves to be ready for new opportunities and are thus able to mobilize quickly to take advantage of them. Anticipating the new with eagerness, we are collectively ready for the adjustments that need to be made to incorporate the change. We are an alive being.

Everyone is interested in learning more and more and the net effect of expending so much energy in learning is that more and better work is getting done. We are talking and communicating more, and the most unlikely pairings of people are discovering common interests. When critical issues arise, the person or unit (we are organized by service units), extends an invitation to whoever can and wants to join the discussion. This has been an incredible way to problem solve, building ownership across the organization. This is a new experience for us, for we used to be very rigid and only know and care about what was happening in our own area of work.

Chaos is normally perceived as destructive to organizational life and therefore to be avoided at all costs. Total avoidance is probably impossible, but at the very least we strive for an alternation between chaos and order, life and death. Such alternation, however, presumes a clear distinction between the pairs. My experience suggests a rather different picture. Chaos and order never appear in purity or isolation, but each is always tending towards the other, and in some real way, includes the other. Organizations without chaos, life without chaos, are impossible, boring, and nonproductive.

I celebrate organizations in "living chaos." Chaos and order, death and birth, now happen so fast, in so many different places, that it all runs in together giving us the fertile field of chaos at all times. Open Space provides the jump-off point for this to happen. I don't believe that order and chaos alternate for life to progress. Rather than looking at this as some kind of cycle (something we can neatly diagram or chart), we need to look at it more like a hologram where formal hierarchial structure coexists with and supports informal structure. In this context, life progresses because order (expressed in the "givens" of an organization) and chaos (all the interactive creativity within our ever changing internal and external environment) are present simultaneously.

Key Ingredients

So... here is what I believe the key ingredients are to sustaining the new and ever renewing after an Open Space event.

➤ *Storytelling*. We take time, on an ongoing basis for storytelling. Telling client stories, stories of our work in relation to our Vision Statement, historical stories, present stories, future stories – this enables expressions of individuality, imagination, the promotion of myth.

➤ *Permission*. An Open Space event permits risk-taking at high levels. But then in getting "back to work" risk-taking feels scary and some people start to apologize for their ideas. Being truthful about the boundaries is a useful antidote. This means being very clear about the "givens" (laws of the land, contract terms, board policy) and essentially being permissive when it comes to everything else. Given this approach, fear decreases, creativity and risk-taking increase, Spirit is enabled, and wonderful stuff happens.

➤ *The Chief Leader*. Leadership happens everywhere, but it is essential not to minimize the critical role played by the chief leader. Needless to say, control style leadership doesn't fit this role. Stories of most tribal chiefs, medicine men, etc., usually reflect that they pay a high personal price in fulfilling their role – if they are any good at all. It takes a lot more personal energy to *enable* than to *control*. *Being present* and being *true over the long haul* is very difficult. For me to achieve and sustain this I must be very intentional about nurturing my own Spirit. My life experiences and learning and my faith commitment have taught me how to do this. I believe that for an organization to sustain Spirit, supporting the "chief" to sustain his or her Spirit is *the* most essential ingredient.

➤ *Spirit*. It has become part of my organization's life to talk about Spirit and welcome Spirit with some common understanding of what it means. When we first talked about Spirit, because we are a church-based organization, people thought we were going "churchy" on them, which really offended some. We needed to work through this, and, in fact, many of those who thought that they wanted nothing to do with Spirit (as in Holy Spirit by their definition) are those who embrace Spirit the most.

➤ *Chaos.* We needed to articulate our understanding of chaos before we could celebrate it and use it, recognizing the difference between Chaos and disorganization. We needed to explore whether there was a difference between individual chaos and organizational chaos. In individual chaos, a person seeks meaning for their life. It was agreed that in the organization, it was the meaning as identified that keeps driving the organization through productive use of Chaos and that this meaning is fostered by critical people in the organization (keepers of the vision).

➤ *Language.* We found that many assumptions/mis-communications occurred because we didn't take the time to teach one another our "language." Most notable were differences in language of senior staff who kept referring to the global picture, supervisory staff who dealt with meeting goals and objectives, and front-line staff who talked about what faced them minute by minute. We all still are passionate about different things based on our role, but we've tried to teach each other our language.

➤ *Appropriate Structure.* I have found that in organizations where people focus on consensus decision making, shared power, putting all their energies into *process* – the organizations eventually are filled with conflict and dysfunction. It is not politically correct to say this, but I rather suspect it is because these organizations are not built on truth – some members are hungry for power and control, but won't say so, others have their "secret agenda" in their breast pocket, but won't clearly put it on the table. In an organization, most power (even to hire and fire) is with the senior staff person, who must claim that power (women have a hard time doing this) and use it wisely and well. For me, this translates into acknowledging that we do and must have a hierarchial structure for some purposes – formal responsibility, accountability, authority, formal communication at the same time that we have and grow an appropriate structure for the actual work of the organization to take place. Both support the other, enable the other, and both are essential and interface with each other.

For further information:
Birgitt Bolton
DALAR Associates
55 Ravinia Crescent.
Ancaster, Ontario L9G 2E8
CANADA
Telephone 905-648-5775

Chapter VI

The University of Kentucky Center for Rural Health

Loyd Kepferle and Karen Main

For reasons remaining somewhat obscure, it turns out that Open Space often migrates from the status of "meeting methodology" toward a new status of, "the way we do business around here." One might assume that an organization doing business in an Open Space mode would accomplish little. That does not seem to be the reality, for Open Space frames the total operation, and internally there is an appropriate alternation between open exploration of new opportunities and predetermined, structured responses to known situations. The key word is "appropriate." In those situations where people know what to do and there are systems in place to take care of that partiucular business, that is the way things work. On the other hand, when novelty is the order of the day, Open Space becomes the dominant mode. The people in Kentucky have been experimenting with all of this, and what follows is a description of their efforts.

The employees of the Center for Rural Health believe that the Center exists as one mechanism for making life better for people who live in rural Kentucky and rural America. These people include our students, our patients, our constituents, and, of course, ourselves. We try to make life better by educating people for better careers in health care, through the health services provided in our clinic, through our community programs which help people improve their health care systems, through research and policy analysis coupled with advocacy for improving health in rural areas, and through programs which will help all of our employees achieve their potential.

The Center is a complex organization functioning within the rules of a much larger bureaucracy to which we are accountable (the University of Kentucky Medical School). While the philosophy enunciated below is one of personal empowerment, we recognize that we are not empowered to act in ways that are contradictory to university rules and regulations. Some of our programs, such as the academic programs, may be more constrained by these rules than others, such as community programs. In addition, while we espouse an egalitarian philosophy, we recognize that for the purposes of accountability, there is an implicit hierarchy within the Center. For example, while employees interested in technology are strongly urged to explore innovations that may help our programs, they will require information from the Center's administrator regarding availability of funds since the administrator is accountable to the director for not overspending the Center's budget. In this example, however, if funds were not available from the Center, this information would only lead the technology group to consider other funding sources. It would not negate their right to improve our programs.

We believe that even with these limitations, the vast majority of problems and opportunities which come to the Center can be resolved by maximizing the talents and creativity of our employees through empowerment. In this regard, we believe that all of us are using our abilities to make the Center Succeed. *All of our contributions are equal.* In these efforts there is no hierarchy or "chain of command." We simply perform different functions.

To operationalize this philosophy, we are working hard to make a process we experimented with a reality in everyday life at the Center. The process is called "Open Space." The main idea of this process is that "People who care most passionately about a problem or opportunity have the *right* and the *responsibility* to do something about it." This basic idea supersedes all notions of a hierarchical organizational structure which requires individuals with problems or ideas to proceed through several layers of authority in order to articulate a problem, solution, or idea before it can be addressed or implemented. Underlying this approach is the idea that *success is dependent on commitment which comes from ownership, which is dependent on power.*

There are only five constraints on this model of personal empowerment: 1. When a problem or opportunity is to be discussed, there must be wide notification of the meeting time and place so that anyone who is interested can attend. 2. Proposed solutions/ideas must be broadcast widely so that they can be acknowledged as Center policies, programs or procedures, or, if they are contradictory to University of Kentucky rules, another solution can be sought. 3. Proposed solutions cannot be hurtful to anyone else. 4. Proposed solutions should channel our limited resources so that they have maximum impact on achieving our goal. 5. Accomplishing the work for which we were hired takes precedence over our group work. However, if the *right* people (those who really care) are involved in any topic, they will find a way to make sure their work is completed and the work of the group is brought to a successful conclusion.

There are *no constraints* on the following: 1. Who can call a meeting. 2. The type of problem or opportunity that is being addressed. 3. The availability of time to have a meeting. 4. Who may attend a meeting. 5. The availability of information necessary for a group to work.

Open Space assumes a consensual process will be observed by the *ad hoc* groups that form and that all ideas will be considered respectfully by the people in the group. Within a group, the convener takes responsibility for articulating the situation under discussion. Another member of the group will act as a recorder. Between the two of them they will develop a brief report of the meeting and circulate it to everyone else at the Center. The *ad hoc* group may choose to modify its plans based on feedback. In this kind of organization there is little reason for an ongoing committee structure. Some groups, for example the academic program heads, may have reason to meet on a regular basis. But we believe committees are most useful if they are composed of people who are really interested in the issue, if they are established to deal with relatively discreet situations, and if they are then dissolved.

While we believe this is a good way to develop a truly successful organization, it is an approach to organizational behavior which is fraught with insecurity which, in the short run, may produce fear, anger, and frustration. It will take a long time for those of us who have lived in hierarchical and paternalistic organizations to believe we are really empowered.

We, at the Center for Rural Health, recognize that this philosophy is somewhat revolutionary and will be uncomfortable to all of us some of the time. But we also believe people do their best when they are empowered to control the conditions that affect them. We also think that solutions which are imposed on people rather than generated by the people who are affected are doomed to failure. Finally, we think we have a wonderful opportunity to test this theory because of the quality of the people who work for the Center. If we are wrong, then, in the spirit of Open Space, we are empowered to throw it out and adopt another philosophy.

For further information:
Loyd Kepferle / Karen Main
Center for Rural Health
100 Airport Garden Drive
Hazzard, Kentucky 41701
USA
Telephone 606-439-3557

Chapter VII

Women's Ways of Leading

Elaine Cornick and Patricia Montgomery

When form and function match, power, effectiveness, and flow are the almost inevitable result. Open Space has been used in a broad range of applications, and each of them brings into focus a different aspect of the approach and its utility in the life of organizations. Occasionally, however, Open Space is used in situations where the match is almost too perfect, at which point it becomes possible to understand both Open Space and the situation in which it was used with greater clarity. Such is the case here.

In 1991, when Sally Helgesen's book *The Female Advantage:Woman's Way's of Leadership* arrived at the bookstores, it caused an immense stir among women in the Portland area. Words jumped out at us, words which acknowledged that maybe we hadn't been doing it all wrong after all – words like collaboration, cooperation, networking, nurturing.

Sally Helgesen bases her book on interviews with four women executives. She found that one of the common principles which informed their leadership style is what she terms the "web of inclusion." This new system is circular; positions are represented as circles, which are then arranged in an expanding series of orbits.

Elaine, as a career counselor, and Patricia, as a college teacher and workshop leader, both work with people in major life transitions and crises. They had noticed for years that women in leadership roles and positions of responsibility often felt "out of sync" with management styles and tended to blame themselves because of the misfit. Clearly there was an audience who needed and wanted to hear a message about women's ways of leading. Doing a conference on this subject was important. Doing an Open Space conference seemed especially appropriate.

The first step was finding the appropriate gathering place. Situated in the Willamette Valley, it was located on 77 acres of woods and meadows, with a lake, wildlife, rolling hills, old forests. Most importantly, a strong feminine energy pervaded the environment: nurturing, abundantly creative, alive, and receptive. THIS WAS THE PLACE!

What is important about this conference is that it evolved through the process of women's ways of leading. The organization and design of the conference was not separate from the content and philosophy of women's leadership; it was a seamless design. Because of this, it was effortless and flowing, organically evolving from the moment of inspiration through the entire weekend, and beyond.

Friends, clients, students, and colleagues shared enthusiasm and delight at the project. The concept of Open Space as a container for the theme of "Women's Ways of Leading" resonated with other women who relished the idea of ambiguity, uncertainty, and lack of structure. Most of all, the co-creative process appealed to them. Before the deadline closed, 26 women had registered.

Preparations for the weekend retreat were important and yet simple: candles, flowers, special items such as crystals and a Goddess figure, a wide range of books for browsing in the library, and music. Elaine walked the perimeter of the grounds, inviting Spirit through ceremony and a meditative presence. Patricia put out flowers and name tags, started some quiet music, lit candles, and then went outside and greeted each woman as she arrived. Each woman introduced herself, reflecting upon these questions: What is something the world knows about you? What is something the world doesn't know about you? The women sang, told stories, reflected on life, and in contentment and completion, retired for bed by midnight.

Following a brief introduction to the Open Space format, the women set to work designing the conference. Within an hour, women scheduled workshops, selected meeting places, and dispersed to their chosen activity.

The discussions covered a wide range of subjects including business and social roles, a new model of the "Emerging Woman," balancing family and work, parenting, politics and gender issues and the "glass ceiling," motherhood, aging, menopause and health issues, and commitment to social and personal change. Spirituality was a core issue throughout the retreat, whether in formal conversation, or in informal talk and play.

What was notable about the day was the gentle ebb and flow of activity and energy. While one core group formed on the patio in the warm summer sunshine, other small groups fluctuated on the perimeter, women moving in and out quietly and without urgency.

In mid-afternoon, nearly all the women had joined or rejoined the original group, with a discussion that was focusing on core issues in women's lives: Who am I? What am I to do with my life? The women's energy seemed to merge, connect, deepen, and strengthen. By late afternoon it felt as if there was one large, harmonious organism.

"I had forgotten what can happen when there are no threatening political or personal ramifications attached to one's thinking and actions. I had dismissed the hope of feeling free to make my own choices based on what I wanted and thought, and acting on them. I thrilled to the experience of being among others in order to exchange personal voices, feelings, processes, knowing that to do so was perfectly right and good, that any expression was welcomed. As the weekend progressed I began to feel what it was like to feel whole and healthy and peaceful inside, and relaxed among others." (Participant)

The conference came to a close after lunch on Sunday with the Talking Stick ritual. The women sat in a circle, each sharing what had touched her, what had meaning for her, and what the gathering meant. Different words, different voices, all expressed an appreciation for the celebration of women's ways of knowing. Some of these statements follow.

"A sense of community, support, and sharing of our women's stories; very powerful and successful, with minimal guidance."

"I felt my own power and contribution."

"I felt that my needs were being met, and that I was taken care of but not controlled."

"I felt heard, understood, and able to explore not-holding-back."

"The weekend was a confirmation of the cooperation and synergy of women."

"It was wonderful playing together as women."

Some women sent written feedback after returning home.

"The key success factor for me was that each woman had stretched herself and experienced some form of leadership in her life. Thus all our energy levels matched without having to be pushed down to accommodate others who hadn't been in leadership positions."

"It was great sharing concentrated time with a group of such strong, healthy, intelligent, and compassionate women, true leaders and role-models of a feminism based in respect for all people, men and women."

"The experience was absolutely life-changing for me. It is my nature to want freedom of movement, thought, and action. It has rarely been my fortune to find it in my living and work conditions. I became so accustomed to accepting a restrictive and dysfunc-

tional style of living and working I was unaware of the inhibited and self-defeating level at which I was functioning until this weekend.

The result of this epiphanous experience was a new resolve to follow my bliss. I want to live my life and offer others the opportunity to live and work in open-ended environments in which they may experience taking the responsibility for their thoughts and actions and come to know what it is like to be validated in a trusting and supportive environment."

"This Open Space method is expansive and stimulates each of us to rise to our potential. When I was a child, I lived in the mountains, and throughout entire summers was able to choose what I would do each day. I learned about spiders, caves, snakes, canoeing; I read books all day; I swam for hours down streams; I rode horses and trusted myself; I trusted that I could handle whatever I chose to do, to learn. And then I lost that quality until this weekend. I found it in the nonthreatening, nonjudgmental Open Space that felt like all the time I needed, all the support I required, and all the inner space I wanted in order to realize that there had been a time, many years ago, when I knew how to live with inner peace, a spirited attitude, and complete trust in myself."

"What I brought home was deep relaxation from a whole-person experience... It was so refreshing to know I was on common ground and among common wisdom about the power – and yes, the responsibility of wise women."

"Not only have I gained trust and respect for others, I have an increased trust and respect for myself, and what I stand for in the world. I have a sense of having joined the larger group of women everywhere who are forging positive changes in society. That new feeling of a positive, powerful membership in a sisterhood that does not seek to exclude men, but rather seeks to unite people, is the greatest blessing I received from this experience."

For further information :
Elaine Cornick or Patricia Montgomery
New Perspectives
1962 NW Kearney / Suite 106
Portland, Oregon 97209
USA
Telephone 503-222-5442

Chapter VIII

Open Space for the Men's Movement

Dick Gilkeson

What is sauce for the goose is sauce for the gander, or so it seems when it comes to the appropriateness of Open Space for the Men's Movement. Just as Elaine Cornick and her sisters discovered that Open Space did marvelous things for their gathering, so also Dick Gilkeson and the brothers. Interestingly, the common point of discovery revolved around a new, or at least a newly perceived, manner of leadership.

Many of those who organize men's events, publish men's journals, or are published themselves, and who otherwise facilitate men's work as part of what has been termed "the men's movement" have been meeting annually for several years. They come together from the continental United States as well as Canada, Great Britain, and Hawaii. Their conferences have been sponsored by Wingspan, the largest men's movement publication, with a quarterly distribution of nearly 150,000.

Robert Bly, whom the press decided must be the leader of the movement, attended the first national conference in 1990. He disavowed the leader role and warned that those who deigned to play it should be prepared to be set up and then discredited by the press. He was very supportive of keeping men's work localized and seemed to share the suspicions others voiced regarding national organizations. Perhaps because of Bly's warning, or maybe because of our own wisdom regarding wanting to change male leadership patterns, historically driven by ego and competitiveness, conference agendas since 1991 have been set by those in attendance only after we arrived at the retreat sites.

Actually the first meeting was also very open. Prior to gathering, each man was asked to contribute to a list of things they wanted to get out of the weekend, as well as a list of things they were bringing to the event. That openness facilitated networking, getting new ideas, developing ideas already made public, and gaining more insight into what the press had labeled "the men's movement." Following a ritual of having men introduce themselves while holding a talking stick, the men self-selected into one of four sessions chosen from their interests described prior to the weekend: men's publications, men's centers or councils, men's events, and where men's work fits versus paid therapy. These sessions were followed by selected group topics, and an open forum. Then a prepared slide show preceded a group-visioning piece and an opportunity to attend a local council meeting.

A wealth of information was shared especially about men's work from one part of the country to another. However, the format encouraged the men to stay in their heads for much of the time, and left several feeling that more needed to be done to facilitate sharing from the heart.

The following year no agenda was announced in advance. The weekend started with an evening rich with ritual. Then all 60 of us were asked to speak in turn about our various visions and interests. From this it became apparent that "leadership" was a topic of broad and significant interest. Without a set agenda it was relatively easy to decide to take up the issue as a group during the weekend.

We uncovered an incredible number of different perspectives. One acknowledged leader of the recovery elements of the movement announced that he was "coming down from the mountain to walk shoulder-to-shoulder with the brothers present." He declared that he was going back into therapy to do some more work on himself and that we shouldn't look to him for leadership. He made a strong plea that we devote our thinking and attention to an "unorganization" and "unleadership," lest we get trapped in our own inflation.

Others made pleas for leaders to step forward, making the case that a leadership void in the movement was irresponsible. Side issues regarding whether what was happening with men was a movement at all, or a group of very different movements, kept the conversation very spirited. I was unable to shake the suggestion that nationally we could, or should, be an unorganization, and that traditional leadership would not serve a vision of a circle of strong, empowered, healing men.

Much of the rest of the weekend consisted of visioning and debating these and related issues as we scripted the agenda, at times, moment to moment with sub-grouping the order of the day. It felt like the kind of Open Space environment I'd been accustomed to in camps I had helped facilitate for adults to address global issues back home. No formal celebration had been planned for Saturday night; nevertheless, we were all treated to one of the grandest of all possible such events: the Northern Lights put on a dazzling show as we stood in sub-freezing temperatures near Ann Arbor, Michigan. The locals said they had never seen such an incredible display of the lights in their collective memories. I was awed and deeply moved. Spirit was definitely present!

At the event just outlined a group announced itself. They described themselves as a networking service agency. Not surprisingly, in an atmosphere of "unleadership" they chose their words carefully. They set themselves up as a national "clearinghouse." They furnished resources. And, they were created to "steward the movement with generativity and brotherhood." "Leadership," of course, was the equivalent of a four-letter word.

What they did not seek to be was, perhaps, even more insightful. To set our minds at rest, they were not a political movement or a controlling agency. They did not advocate or practice centralization or hierarchical structures. They were not exclusionary. And, they did not "presume to speak for men in general or the men's movement." What could be less threatening?

The first packet of information the group handed out included Robert K. Greenleaf's visionary writings on "servant leadership," based on his understanding of the importance of the servant Leo in Hermann Hesse's *Journey to the East*. The 2-year-old Servant Leadership School on Columbia Road in the Adams Morgan area of Washington, D.C., has trained thousands already in the style of leadership advocated by Greenleaf. For those not familiar with servant leadership, perhaps it is easiest to describe it as leadership that serves its constituency or community with vision and purposeful action as contrasted to "ego" leadership, which is based on "what I want," or "my needs."

Greenleaf wrote that it is hard for a group with a large task or mission to trust ego leadership because of its inherent "hidden agenda." On the other hand, groups will unite around a servant leader whom they sense is willing to take any task, empower any member of the group, and labor wholeheartedly with compassionate disinterest for the good of the entire group.

He also wrote that a mature community is ever vigilant to the sniff of ego leadership, its blatant or subtle manifestations, and its telltale bramble thicket of ego/power issues which block the community from flowing into the future. Where dissension, chronic conflict, and agenda with a capital "A" reign, we can be certain that ego leadership, rather than servant leadership is prevailing. The world will long remember those who came to us as servants: Gandhi, Martin Luther king, Jr., Mother Teresa, and the rest. Those who would bend and twist the souls of others for their own self-seeking and personal status fulfillment will soon be discredited or forgotten.

More importantly, this group captured the sentiment I heard expressed in one way or another by any number of men at the '91 conference. Heaven help the man who would deign to be the "leader" of the men's movement in this country. And heaven help the man or men who would try to build a national organization, other than one set up to facilitate, but not control, networking.

The men from Seattle volunteered to host the 1992 Wingspan conference. Their challenge was much clearer than it had been for previous hosts. How were they to put on a successful conference where significant work would get done, and important decisions made, if no one was to be the leader in the traditional sense? Too much structure might be interpreted as an attempt at control. That male trait was clearly taboo. And *laissez faire* was a prescription for chaos – also not acceptable when planning for men to meet who were paying over $1000 for round-trip airfare. Fortunately, the seeds for a successful conference for an unled unorganization had already been laid.

  Robert Carlson, the man who headed up the Seattle conference planning group, was a man of strict democratic and consensual values. He and two other men had created and facilitated the Seattle Men's Wisdom Council for 7 years. The Council had grown to roughly 250 men who met once a month to drum and then to address given topics using a process created by marrying the anonymity and safety of 12-step processes, the speaking from the heart present in Quaker Meetings, and the fairness of passing a talking stick familiar to many native American rituals. The talking stick allowed the speaker to be heard without interruption. This process also banned crosstalk, such that the man stating his truth need not fear being judged.

  Little wonder that Robert had stumbled across Open Space in looking for a way to carry out the conference. The invitation allowed only that we would meet and set the agenda in Open Space once we all assembled. Since essentially that's what we had done the year before, I doubt that the invitation was very controversial. I also doubt that few men knew the significance of formalizing the conference process by referring to Open Space. I did. And I was delighted.

For me it was to be the perfect marriage of a conference technology to a loosely webbed non-organization that encouraged servant leadership. I arrived at the conference expecting once again to be filled with the spirit of Open Space. Then I discovered that the term was to be used to bless the process of starting without an agenda. Beyond that, and a planned celebration for Saturday night, little else had been formalized.

The conference leaders had planned to take those who wished to attend their monthly Wisdom Council meeting into Seattle on Saturday morning. Less than half the group chose to go with them, leaving the majority of the group at the retreat site. The group that stayed behind was eager to go to work. Fortunately, before retiring on Friday, Robert had asked me if I and another man, and anyone else we might choose, would lead the group staying behind. The other man volunteered to lead a morning ritual to get us grounded and started. I said that I would use the opportunity to introduce a more formalized Open Space process.

I was used to working with flip chart paper to have those who wanted to lead sessions post their offerings, proposed time slots, locations, and sign ups. When I went to round up the flip charts on Saturday morning I was told there were none. The thought occurred to me that there might be some actual butcher paper in the kitchen. Voila! There was indeed! I knew we'd have been able to use tablet paper, but being able to announce that we'd be using actual butcher paper was much more useful in putting everyone at ease.

After briefly describing the origins of Open Space (value of coffee breaks, letting go of outcomes, etc.), and suggesting that we had been evolving to such a process, I had the 50 men begin the agenda-setting process. Actually the process had already been superbly started by Carlson the night before when he suggested that each man introduce himself by describing the passion that had been the reason for their joining this conference. Translating those passions to suggested sessions proved an easy task and we were through the chaos of the agenda setting and negotiating process regarding the morning Open Space easily within 15 minutes. The actual sessions were as thought-provoking and stimulating as any I have attended in other Open Space conferences. I now take that part of the process for granted.

When the men were asked what they wanted to do that afternoon, they kicked possibilities around for a few minutes and then one fellow said that the process I had led had been very useful and that I should do it again for them. That suggestion was quickly seconded and adopted and we headed for the butcher paper again. I sensed that the process was working very well once again by the men I saw moving from group to group as they used their feet to take responsibility for their learning.

Unfortunately, the men decided that they did not want to have evening news. They'd been bored the year before by report-outs. So we informally passed on what we had done in our various sub-groups, had a marvelous salmon feast for dinner complete with hula dancing by two Hawaiian men who were present, and settled in to a night of celebrating with drums and other exotic instruments, storytelling, and poetry.

Sunday's agenda brought us all back together again and we loosely described in turn our visions for where men's work was going. After this we closed with an appropriate ritual, accompanied by a display of thunder and lightning – a rarity in the Northwest, and a sure sign that Spirit was again present. I promised to forward information about Open Space to the men who were most interested.

As might have been predicted, the men felt we got a lot accomplished in a highly charged spiritual atmosphere. I volunteered to host a Portland Regional conference the following year, and was well supported. Naturally, we used Open Space technology, the method most of the men probably feel they invented. I have little doubt that it is the ideal conferencing technology for the unorganization, which remains mostly unled, which is already providing a viable alternative for creating the communities that will ensure the survival of the planet in the next century.

For further information:
Dick Gilkeson
The MidPoint
16448 NW McNamee
Portland, Oregon   97231-2104
USA
Telephone 503-621-3612

Chapter IX

Eur-Open Space I

Christopher Schoch

For reasons unclear, there is a continuing perception that Open Space will not quite work in Europe. The conservative traditions of the continent, to say nothing of control-oriented hierarchical organizations, supposedly create an unfavorable environment for Open Space. The truth, however, is somewhat different. In fact, one of the first uses of Open Space in a real live organization (as opposed to an experimental group) was with the Accor Group of France, one of the largest hospitality corporations in the world. Not only did Open Space find a receptive place in the world of Accor, but has been used on a annual basis for Accor's senior executive university program. Christopher Schoch tells the story.

After several years of working together and corresponding with Harrison Owen, it occurred to us that experience with Open Space in Europe was limited and probably not very well known; so, I was quite happy to accept Harrison's invitation to submit this article. May I begin by saying that my work in OS has almost entirely been done in France (albeit with very international groups), and this article draws heavily from that Gallic experience.

The Accor Experience: Background

As head of international training at Accor's corporate university "l'Academie," it was my modest task to help satisfy the training needs for the overseas divisions of this major service giant which today employs 147,000 people in 68 countries throughout the world. One of my major initiatives took place in 1990 when I organized the first week-long Corporate Summer University which brought together some 65 senior managers from the international hotel, restaurant, service voucher, and tourism businesses. By mid-week we knew that things had gone well because we (the organizers) were exhausted, and they (the participants) were still present and busily moving through the agenda of planned talks, panels, and workshops. The evaluation forms showed that overall satisfaction was high. Our biggest problem seemed to be how we could possibly do as well, or better, next time – hopefully with less stress and fatigue.

A day or two later I ran into one of the North American managers who had attended the event. He immediately assuaged my doubts. "Look", he said, "you guys did a great job. And that's just the point – you did too much. We (the Accor managers) are a bunch of very busy guys, who seldom get a chance to share all of the passionate work we are doing all over the world – why not just give us the floor for awhile and let us just get together." Deep down I had to concede that something indeed very basic was wrong – not with the organization, but with the art form. Doing better next year was no longer the issue: we would have do things *differently*, something that could capitalize on the richness and diversity of Accor's group of managers.

Participation became my obsession, as I searched for a new way to bring together a hundred or so managers. (Our success had almost doubled the demand for attendance.) It was my friend Manfred Mack (a Paris-based author and consultant) who talked to me about Open Space. "If you really want to do something different you must get in touch with Harrison Owen." He didn't believe that anything more participative could be found this side of heaven or hell.

When I first spoke on the phone to Harrison, I learned that we had common spiritual roots, having both worked in West Africa in the '60's with the Peace Corps. After listening to him for only a few minutes I intuitively felt that we were going to end up doing something together. That first conversation convinced me that Open Space was exactly what could do the trick for our 1991 Summer University, and I decided to go with it

Nineteen ninety-one was to be another year of record profit for Accor and a year targeted for new expansion. But with the Gulf War and its aftermath, only the latter proved to be true. Motel 6 had been acquired the year before, making Accor the world leader in the economy hotel line with more than 800 hotels owned and managed. By March, long months of negotiating led to the first stage of agreement with Wagon Lits that would eventually lead in November to Accor's takeover of this large Belgian holding company with majority control of a wide portfolio of companies in different service branches including hotels, railcar services, industrial catering, car rentals, and travel agencies. The agreement called for Accor to take over the management of three major hotel chains in the two-star (Arcade), three-star (Althea), and four-star (Pullman) ranges. In less than 8 months Accor had become the world's leading hotel operator, adding 400 units to its already impressive network of chains, with a yet unspecified involvement in the other areas of Wagons Lits business. Added to the Motel 6 acquisition, Accor had doubled its business surface and was virtually a new company. Moreover, 40% of its new employee base were coming from company cultures that contrasted sharply with the bold, decentralized, entrepreneurial style cultivated over the years by Accor founders and co-chairmen, Paul Dubrule, and Gerard Pelisson. Suddenly the theme of the Summer University, *The New World of Accor: Learning and Building Together* took on special meaning, and the introduction of Open Space seemed to fit in perfectly at a moment of historical transition for the group.

    The Summer University was scheduled for the first week of July. In mid-April, Harrison came for the first time to the Academie Accor in Evry (a "Ville Nouvelle" 20 miles south of Paris), where Accor also has its worldwide headquarters. A series of meetings with the training and human resource people, and the managers, enabled Harrison to tell the story of Open Space, answer questions, and create interest and support for Open Space, which is a far cry from the French rational control, Cartesian mode of thought and organization. It was then also that, coached by Harrison, we solved the venue problem. The Academie, although a modern training facility with over 10 meeting rooms, had no single room that could accommodate more than 60 people in a conventional format. We decided that the event would have to take place "on campus" in a tent that would be mounted for the occasion. As things turned out, this was to be a key decision.

By early May, enrollment was launched through a letter announcing only the theme and purpose of the meeting, a few words on Open Space, and the dates. Our target was a broad range of international senior managers. Executive committee members were also personally invited to attend. The response was enthusiastic, particularly from the newly acquired management staffs, and we ended up with more than 100 attendees from 22 different countries, of whom more than 40 came from Wagon Lits. For many it would be their first major encounter with Accor people. A score of brand CEOs and general managing directors also signed up. We now had the ingredients for a very interesting and even dramatic event: diversified population, high common purpose, and Open Space (or *high learning* as Harrison would call it).

An Historic First

On Friday afternoon attendees trickled into the Academie and were encouraged to mount displays of their brands or countries in the large tent that had taken 3 days to mount. The tent itself was impressive – not just any tent mind you, but a very aesthetic, draped enclosure that looked more like a sheik's desert palace than a circus tent. It rose from within the confines of the gardens, formed by the interior walls of the U-shaped building which houses the Academie. The tent softened the rather harsh modern architecture of that brick structure, and opened enticingly out from the windows of the mezzanine. The Academie had been almost magically transformed and there was an atmosphere of excitement and anticipation. There was also some apprehension from the Academie trainers, some of whom had volunteered to be reporters. They seemed concerned that Open Space was too American to work in France, and couldn't imagine letting 100 people loose for 2 whole days without trained facilitators or instructors to keep them within bounds.

Following a welcome "aperitif," everyone was invited to come to the tent for opening remarks. People gathered in a circle around the two co-chairmen, who were not accustomed to the format but graciously accepted to provide a warmer, more intimate atmosphere. The chairmen spoke confidently of the company's future and encouraged the attendees to join them in facing the challenges of a newly aligned management team. In so doing they had implicitly given their permission to enter into Open Space, which is of considerable importance in Latin countries, such as France, which place much importance on loyalty to the company and its leaders.

On Saturday, a slate of speakers addressed various strategic issues. The president of Wagons Lits made an impassioned plea to welcome Accor's new colleagues from his company with respect and an open mind. The president of Motel 6 compared Accor's takeover of his company to other takeovers that he had experienced with very mixed results in the USA. Harrison Owen talked about Chaos, Manfred Mack about new trends in management, and Yan De Stael, a communications consultant, about the importance of image and identity. The rather long day for the participants helped reframe some of the immediate problems of Accor, such as transition and integrating people in the new organizations. The stage was well set for launching Open Space on the following day, a Sunday.

At this point I would like to share an anecdote that provides another example of the inter-cultural dynamics that accompany running Open Space in France. On Friday morning Harrison and I discovered that the main wall, our "agenda" for Open Space, was covered with a floating layer of light blue cloth that perfectly matched the dark blue carpet and drapes that adorned the corners of the tent. It was lovely, an awkward surface on which to tape the meeting sign-up sheets, but lovely to look at. A great debate ensued during which the American virtue of practicality clashed strongly with the French virtue of esthetics. Harrison and I preferred taking the cloth off, exposing a rough-surfaced plywood wall – not so pretty, but easier to tape and move sheets of paper on. After having spent 2 days of mounting and decorating the tent with great attention, our French friends were deeply offended by the ugliness of our proposition. Just as frustration seemed to lead to an impasse, I suggested that perhaps the boards could be painted over in time for our Sunday morning launching of Open Space. The French agreed to this as long as the cloth could remain for the Friday meeting with the co-chairmen (anything perceived as unesthetic can draw public rebuke in France). Saturday night the painters went to work and by Sunday morning at 9:00am the paint on the wall was just barely dry. Cardboard and crepe paper butterflies and bumblebees adorned the tent and Harrison proceeded to welcome everyone to Open Space as I translated.

Harrison seemed to understand that Accor, and French organizations in general, have a highly competitive spirit. When he mentioned that perhaps this group would break the speed record for organizing the village market place, he ignited a spark that led to an intense and rapid response. In only a few brief moments 15 people were standing in the circle with their sign-up sheets ready. In less than 20 minutes, more than 30 ideas had been proposed, and the tent was buzzing as people clustered at the wall to organize their 2 days. Any doubts that the participants would respond spontaneously to Open Space in a French cultural setting (more conducive to formal and highly rehearsed presentations) were dispelled. However, not all doubts were dispelled that the meeting would not somehow end in disaster.

When some semblance of calm had returned to the tent, and most of the participants had broken into their meetings, one of the Academie trainers ran up to me nervously. "Well, as I expected, it just isn't working." she said. She explained that about 20 participants were watching TV and among them, the most senior members of the group. She was quite upset and convinced that they were defying me, Harrison, Open Space, and the Academie's authority. Well, France is the country of "La Bastille," noted for its rebelliousness and reluctance to accept authority from the "Anglo-Saxons" so I felt I should go to the scene of the "uprising" – with some degree of anxiety I must admit. I was only about one hour into my first Open Space event: could this be my first unpleasant surprise? Harrison had only mentioned enthralling surprises, like nudity, or joyful serendipity – he had never talked about Open Revolt.

When I found the dissident group, they were sitting silently and reverently in front of the television set totally engrossed in the French Grand Prix formula one auto race. It was like stumbling into a chapel during Mass, so I respectfully withdrew and left our senior executives to their spiritual communing. I thought to myself: well in Open Space the only law is the Law of Two Feet and they were obeying it rigorously, so no one has anything to say or do about it.

Later on that morning one of the people who had been watching the race told me, "I saw you when you came up to the TV room. What you should know is that when the race was over, we all turned around and looked at each other. Someone asked what the fact that we were all there passionately watching the same event tells us about Accor. We had a lively exchange, after which many of us concluded that we had shared many things that were related to formula one racing (Accor's European economy hotel chain happens to be called "Formula 1.") Then I went to a discussion," he continued, "and I must say that I got very involved; some fantastic things came out of it. If I hadn't been able to watch the race, I don't think my participation would have been very good." This manager of a major hotel brand had just provided me a wonderful demonstration of the dynamics of the law of two feet.

Those familiar with Open Space events know that there is a rising collective consciousness as the participants discover and explore new ideas, new synergies, new relationships and ways of relating to one another. An Accor spirit was unfolding, or "Esprit d'Accor" as Harrison had named it early on. The people from Wagon Lits were discovering a tolerant, dynamic group of people that placed a high degree of trust in one another. Open Space was not only revealing the potential of Accor and Wagon Lits people to come together, it was also shaping their common identity.

An evaluation of the 2 days brought out more than 40 different discussions, on a wide array of topics: the implementation of the Sofitel-Pullman management merger, how the Academie Accor could better serve the needs of international divisions, the need for Accor to develop its image, the right to dissent, a proposition to develop corporate citizenship, how Accor could bring together its competencies in hotels, and Wagons Lits' competencies in train catering to create a new hospitality concept. If there was an overriding theme it was a blend of creativity, opening up, and developing a more top-line (or people oriented) approach to business. The director of the Academie estimated that Accor had gained six months to one year in the merging process with Wagons Lits, whose people came away convinced they had a role to play in Accor and that the culture encouraged them to express their opinions. The feeling coming away from the Open Space work during the Summer University was one of optimism. Invisible organizational barriers had been overcome and the participants were surprised at how much untapped creativity emerged from the experience. One group dedicated to Corporate Citizenship decided to meet and draft a charter for Accor, addressing the issues of job opportunity for handicapped persons, environmental responsibility in purchasing, and support for artists.

This group eventually met with the co-chairmen and saw their draft adopted as policy. As a result of their work in Open Space, three hotel brands decided to set up corporate citizenship committees.

Though the chairmen, Pellisson and Dubrule, did not attend the Open Space meeting, they were certainly surprised to encounter so much enthusiasm from those who had. The power of Open Space was recognized by the fact that several merged hotel brands scheduled their own OS events to accelerate the blending process and develop a new identity for their management staffs.

Can Lightening Strike Twice in Open Space?

When time came around to thinking about the '92 summer university, some at the Academie felt that lighting should not strike twice in the same place. Their argument was that although Open Space was novel, it couldn't ever be as effective and powerful as the first time, and would only produce disappointment for those who had attended the first one. Besides, Harrison Owen was no longer available for the chosen dates, and many were convinced that Open Space could be brought about only through his very personal and unique magic.

In early 1992 Accor was still busy digesting its joint management of the Wagon Lits Hotels, with a lot of management changes and new organizations. Nineteen ninety-one had not been a good year but 1992 was off to an even worse start. Nonetheless confidence was still strong that the Group would ride the waves and come out with its strategy and business intact. The decision was made to stay close to the previous year's theme and frame in the context of the 500th anniversary of Columbus' famous discovery: *Beyond Our Borders: Exploring Together the New Opportunities of Change.*

The theme in fact was the borderless organization as a response to globalization and organizational transformation. To help us Noel Tichy, of the University of Michigan was asked to set up a workshop on global competition, and the CEO of Phillips, Yan Timmer, was invited as special guest speaker on transformation and leadership.

Open Space was also retained, following my insisting that its major advantage was as a learning process for networking. In fact we upped the ante by bringing computerized conferencing into the meeting in the hope of extending Open Space dynamics beyond the event and carrying the networking effect one step further than the previous year.

One big event was to mark Accor in 1992 and certainly for many years beyond. Accor successfully launched a takeover bid for majority ownership of the Wagon Lits holding company. The two co-chairmen suddenly found themselves at the head of an empire which included car rentals, railway catering, and travel agencies, businesses in which it had no previous experience. Accor had gone from a position of underleveraged debt, to one where few people inside could see how it would be able to continue financing the development of its traditional hotel businesses.

Open Space Blows Off the Lid

The Summer University came at a time of great internal soul searching and during the two day Open Space session, ably launched by Manfred, the lid literally blew off. Passionate discussions of up to 50 people tried to identify a new global strategy for the group in increasingly difficult European markets. Calls for forceful leadership were expressed, and several meetings actually plotted out change strategies for the older brands and particularly Novotel ("Is it possible to change a 25-year-old product?"). There was a ground surge of desire for corporate renewal; clearly the 175 participants (including the top 20) were asking for stronger leadership and guidance from the co-chairmen. To bring those messages home, a self-appointed 5-member committee including the director of the Academie, the vice president of human resources, the chief legal advisor, the head of North American operations, and the chief of staff, met and drafted a summary of the meaning and results of Open Space.

In the early days of September, two very determined co-chairmen called a press conference and announced a "cultural revolution." Accor was facing serious challenges that required immediate response. Too many people had become complacent, and now the company would expect each person to justify his contribution to the company's goals. Headquarters would become leaner, and in general people would have to run scared.

They also set up a new organization: independent brand development would be curtailed, and new internal alliances sought. Pay increases for senior management staff would be granted for

1993 only on a case-by-case basis. All this was in direct response to demands for stronger leadership that came out clearly from the 1992 Open Space meeting.

"Play it again Harrison"

I will at this point sumarize briefly the third consecutive Open Space – Summer University meeting by saying that once again the question was asked: "Can it work again?" The management of the Academie agreed to keep it in the design, but asked that it be reduced to one day for economic reasons. The '93 theme was *The Spirit of Service* which really was an invitation to look at what was at the core of Accor's business in terms of customer commitment and the quality of hospitality. Open Space work was more devoted to the role of management, bringing customers into the decision making process, and developing fundamental service values inside the organization. My Benedictine friend, Father Huges Minguet, gave a very moving talk on what the world's oldest (1500 years) hospitality multi-national (The chain of Benedictine monasteries) had learned about the trade. This, together with Charles Handy's workshop on the future of quality in organizations, provided timely inspiration to the 180 participants. The 32 reports were of a very creative and penetrating nature, and raised issues that are still providing fuel to Accor's continued drive for corporate renewal.

Three Years of Open Space: The Bottom Line

If I try to evaluate the impact of Open Space and the Summer University after 3 years, the following results are obvious to me:

➤ Accor's whole approach to communication has been affected. Corporate identity is now developed as a permanent program called "Esprit Accor" – thank you Harrison. Open Space has revealed the collective strengths of an otherwise loosely bound organization.

➤ It has served as a forum and voice for change for those in a very large organization where, as in all large organizations, the tendency is to "kill the messenger." This has been hard to do when there are 175 or so messengers every year proposing not only to support change but to lead it when necessary. It allowed Accor's major hotel brands to engineer change at least one year earlier than they would have.

➤ As a process it has led many brands to adopt empowerment into their management, and I can directly refer to the Courte Paille restaurant chain (for whom I facilitated a 2 day event for all of its managers); the Arche roadside restaurant chain (which has run an ongoing series of Open Space meetings for its employees); Novotel, Sofitel, Motel 6 (all of whom have run Open Space operations of one kind or another).

Open Space has now been retained as a permanent part of the Summer University – or at least until further notice, which is about as much commitment you can get from a company as mobile as Accor.

The most rewarding testimony for me came at the concluding meeting of last year's Open Space, which was attended for the first time by both co-chairmen. It was a powerful experience to participate in a free-flowing dialogue in which participants could share what they had learned from the meeting and ask the two chairmen questions. In reply to a young lady's question "Mr. President what is Accor for you?" Gerard Pellison (who is noted as being very bottom line) said, *"This is Accor,"* making a sweeping gesture that included the tent and its occupants. "I don't think I have found a better example of what Accor means than what you have done here together these last days," he concluded. After 3 years Open Space had finally been defined as concomitant to Accor's federated, networked organization, not by me but by the co-chairman himself.

The Transcultural Dynamics of Open Space

The Accor Summer University Open Space experience is the most enduring that I have seen introduced in France, but it is not the only one. I facilitated Open Space events and meetings for several other Accor brands, as well as for other organizations including a commercial bank, a network of consultants, church parishes, and the Catholic national relief agency. These experiences have led me to understand that in order for Open

Space to work in France, a number of cultural parameters must be taken into account that one would not necessarily encounter in the United States, but which may apply more generally to Europe.

In France (as in Spain, Belgium, Italy, Portugal, and Germany) people are accustomed to accepting unequal distribution of power, and relatively little interaction between different social levels in a normal organizational setting. Thus the decision of whom to invite as well as the role of hierarchy requires much greater attention than in countries like the US and Denmark. Most managers and CEOs believe that if you mix management levels, members of lower rank will automatically be dominated by the more senior people. So the CEO, and in some cases, the executive committee most often refrain from participating directly in Open Space, choosing instead to come before or after the Open Space meeting. The danger here is that senior management may feel outflanked on issues that they were not able to work on during the meeting, and thus may squelch new ideas or initiatives.

To reduce this danger I always insisted that the CEO, or leader, prepare a kind of state of the union address which is meant to set the tone and indicate just how far people may explore the subject of the meeting. Also, I prepare carefully with them the closing session during which I put things into perspective by analyzing the trends of the Open Space discussions. Having a third party view of the content and process takes some of the pressure off a CEO who might otherwise be tempted to react negatively to certain ideas or discussions, taking them out of their context.

It is important that the meeting be seen as contributing to company strategy, which of course must be clear to the participants. Open Space often provides an excellent opportunity for senior management to review and clarify strategy. Using the same logic, whatever comes out of Open Space should also be framed back into the strategy even if the announced or prevailing strategy is brought under criticism. In fact the French, who can sometimes appear to be highly critical, are surprisingly constructive in Open Space to which they have invariably responded well in my experience.

Culture also affects the way people use or don't use the law of two feet. In France one would never leave a meeting conducted by his boss just because he wasn't getting anything out of it. In southern European cultures, group interests are given the priority over individual interests, a potential inhibitor of the law of two feet. Europeans, therefore, need more time to feel really comfortable in Open Space, as well as more elaborate, polite forms of leave taking. There are fewer bumblebees in Europe than in the USA, and more "Bernaches" (Geese – which is what Harrison called those who "stay in formation" until the leader adjourns the discussion). As Geert Hofstede also points out in his work on cultural dimensions on organizations, cultures which encourage people to "stay in formation" tend to discourage work in task forces, or small autonomous groups. People from "southern European cultures" (with the notable exception of Italians) can feel uncomfortable in situations where hierarchy is not clearly defined and the focus is exclusively on getting things done or moving outside of the scope of the official organization. Obviously this factor affects the way people perceive the validity of the informal discussion groups that Open Space spawns. In France there is real concern whether or not these groups will be taken seriously by the official structure since they have no real authority, or authorship (empowerment to initiate "legislation" or proposals on behalf of the organization).

Another cultural parameter affecting Open Space concerns attitudes and beliefs on change. In many European countries change and novelty are not accepted as inherently desirable – as they are in North America. Social process experimentation in France is viewed with reserve. The idea that individuals can and should take responsibility for their future is not widespread. The French tend rather to believe that hierarchy, and management, with much more arbitrary use of power than Americans or Canadians are accustomed to, should be responsible for improving or changing the organization.

In conclusion, more time and discussion must go into an Open Space project before the sponsors, be they managers or function specialists, will feel comfortable with Open Space. But if you take that time and accept French cultural sensitivity as perfectly legitimate, working in Open Space (we call it "Eur-Open Space") can be very rewarding.

For further information:
Christopher Schoch
20, Bd. De la République
92210 Saint Cloud, FRANCE
Telephone 33-1-69-36-90-06

Chapter X

Open Space: An Organization Transition Methodology

Hugh Huntington

Hugh Huntington lives in Taos, New Mexico, but he is quite likely to show up almost anywhere. A number of years ago, I was walking down a forest path on a relatively deserted Maine Island. When I reached a crossing there was Hugh. That may be significant, because Hugh does seem to show up at the crossing points of my life. That has certainly been the case with Open Space. I think it is fair to say that Hugh approached Open Space with a high degree of scepticism. Most of his prior experience as a trainer and consultant suggested that it wouldn't, or perhaps, shouldn't work. But it did, and it does. All of which caused Hugh to rethink some basic premises.

A large avionics defense plant was in two major transitions. The first was a down-sizing from 2400 to 1600 people, reflecting the cutback in Department of Defense (DOD) expenditures. The second was a total reorganization from a traditional, autocratic management system that reflected both internal corporate philosophy and DOD expectations to a team-based structure. This meant the removal of four of the seven levels of management and supervision within the plant. The switch to the new organizational structure was to begin in 3 weeks, to be completed within 8 weeks.

Management had made a commitment to their corporate office to move ahead.

Because of my previous work teaching team-building within the plant at senior and middle-levels of management, I was asked to review the reorganization plan for potential problems. While this type of transition involves many unknowns, I had two major concerns: the first was the lack of a definition of purpose for a group of internal experts whose services were required by various teams; the second was a complete absence of planning or training to help individuals make the transition from an autocratic to a team-based mindset, with its accompanying behaviors.

Traditional forms of team-based instruction were not feasible from a time and cost standpoint. Instead, Open Space Technology was recommended as a method to help the plant make the transition. Open Space was not represented as a method to address all of the issues, nor to teach all of the team-based skills that would be required, but rather as a process that would result in essential team behavior experiences. Open Space is used to enhance communication, establish communication links where needed, teach people the process of listening, and help them learn the fundamentals of self-empowerment.

Approximately 450 of the 1600 employees in the plant participated in a total of 16 Open Space processes. The manufacturing area was the only one where lower-level employees were not included in the process in large numbers. All other departments brought the vast majority, if not the total group, to the Open Space session. Only one senior manager decided not to use Open Space in her department (finance and accounting). This decision was based on the manager's personal experience with a previous plant-wide Open Space; she found it very difficult to tolerate the silence in the group during the session and concluded that it was essentially unproductive. She also found herself in a political bind because her department reported directly to corporate management and her boss did not like the idea of the conversion to a team-based organizational structure.

The results of Open Space ranged from outstanding to mediocre. One group, in a 2 day session, reorganized itself, determined how to maintain the existing functions, established priorities for work assignment, determined how emergency production situations would be handled, selected team leaders, determined how the team leaders would function in the team council, and on what basis the team council chairperson would be selected and rotated. During this session they also decided to physically relocate themselves to the present area of the plant using their own time and labor, as there was no money in the budget available for that move. The manager of this group described himself as an ex-Marine with an extremely strong, autocratic leadership style. With great difficulty, but intense commitment, he undertook the task of letting his group assume the responsibility for itself. Three months after his 2 day Open Space session he said, "I used to think that in all my years of experience I had learned how to control people who worked for me. I now have more control than I've ever had in my life and I'm doing much less to get it. Through Open Space people have come to function as a team that needs little or no daily direction from me."

At the other end of the success spectrum lie two frustrations. The first was a group without a clear definition of role or ego satisfaction relative to the new structure. It was extremely difficult to have them generate enthusiasm within an Open Space session. This group was responsible for all the high-powered thinking and expertise required to produce the range of sophisticated products manufactured in this plant. They were primarily high-tech, research employees who had always had their priorities set for them by senior management. Their expertise was called on, based on 32 different team leaders' assessments of a need for their skills. Three months into the organizational redesign, many of these people were still not clear about what their jobs were. They felt unneeded and unwanted; they were depressed and despondent and many of them left the plant for different employment.

To compound this situation, the group manager, despite his constructive and energetic intent, was not able to stop providing answers to questions developed in the small break-out sessions. This continually undermined any sense of self-direction that the group was beginning to generate. While the session would not be considered a failure, the hurdles seemed too high for this group to overcome to make this session work well.

The second group with relatively mediocre results was the manufacturing group. The manager of this group stated his belief in and commitment to a transition to teams, but he moved so slowly that his group began to mistrust his intent. I believe that deep within this man's heart, he did believe what he said, but his fear and intense autocratic background (including a Naval

Academy education) led him to keep tight controls on his teams. Other groups that needed to interact with his group had initial doubts about his intent; after 6 months they distrusted his group completely. During the Open Space sessions with this group there was a large reluctance to say what needed to be said. The problems defined were of sufficient magnitude that enormous discussion could have been held, but the group was unwilling to come to decision or commit to the resolution of various issues. The fear of the boss's autocratic leadership style was the primary cause of their reluctance.

The senior-level management group, originally 13 people, made the decision to switch to a team-based structure. During the reorganization those 13 were reduced to 7; only 2 of those remained 18 months after the switch to teams. The plant manager, who still remains, said at the end of the Open Space work, "I have just begun to understand what we have designed and created. Behaviors required to function in teams are radically different than anything I ever perceived."

One enthusiastic manager volunteered to lead her group in an Open Space process as soon as the organizational transition had taken place. Twelve people were eventually trained to run Open Space within the plant, but only five of those twelve ever actually conducted Open Space sessions. By the time they were trained, the internal realities of political and hierarchical expectations had become clear; it was more difficult to work the Open Space process within groups where management had not made a full commitment to the team-based structure. In all other major groups where a commitment had been made, Open Space worked extremely well and the group knew how to move forward with it on their own.

What became immediately obvious was the difference between individuals who were willing to commit to teams and those who believed "this too shall pass," or were sensitive to the political alignments required by various managers. As one person reflected, "No one escaped Open Space."

Perhaps the greatest and longest-lasting impact was on individuals who made a strong investment in the Open Space process. During the making of a video documentary on the impact of Open Space within this plant, the testimony about changes in self-image as a result of the Open Space experience were not only numerous but exceeded any I had ever observed in classic team-building programs. Many individuals commented on the transfer of what they had learned into their family, church, and civic organizations. While no one used a full Open Space structure, Open Space principles brought enormous change wherever they were applied.

Large numbers of people commented on how differently they listened after experiencing Open Space; they realized that they had never really known how to listen well before. They also understood when they were or were not being listened to. Many people commented on the incredible change in communication with individuals that they had known for a long period of time, and a new ability to establishment communication links with people that they had not worked with before.

Team-based structures require that people act with empowerment; those people who invested themselves in the process of Open Space learned the empowerment lesson, and learned it well. The difference between senior managers who were willing to support empowered employees and those who gave only lip service became obvious to the casual observer almost immediately. Management philosophies that were incongruent with actions also became obvious. Several managers reported intense satisfaction and a radical alteration of their management philosophies based on what they had learned.

Many individuals took on more responsibility for what was happening in the plant. Though this process was slow and difficult, Open Space made it clear that the assumption of individual responsibility was absolutely necessary if a team-based organization was to succeed.

Perhaps one of the biggest surprises was that, as a result of experiencing the Open Space, people quickly moved through the grieving process for the loss of their old job identity, the loss of some friends to the down-sizing as well as friends who chose to not be a part of the team structure, and the loss of their old application of skills and knowledge. They also moved through the fear and anxiety of learning to work in entirely new positions within the organization. One group spent the first 2 of the 3 day Open Space griping, blaming, and talking about "they." By the end of the third day they realized that the word "they" was used only when blame or denial of responsibility was taking place. As one person said, "When we came to understand that, there was no place to hide."

Implications for Training and Organizational Development

In many cases the assumption that team behaviors would be demonstrated and learned in the process of Open Space proved true beyond our wildest expectations. Five of the 12 people trained to do Open Space within the plant had backgrounds and training in organizational development. They frequently left at the end of the day in a state of shock at what they had observed. Questions being asked in every Open Space were, "What's really going on here?" and "How can this be happening?" They were referring to the tremendous speed, clarity, and intensity of communication among participants in Open Space. To the person, they all said that they had never been able to create, in their best training and organizational development processes, the level of interaction occurring within these groups.

When we stepped back to review what some individuals learned about themselves, we came to see that their whole self-image around their role in the organization had changed radically. People who had seen themselves only as insignificant workers realized that they could have a major impact on their group, and in some cases, on the plant itself. Others learned to take courage where they never dreamed it was possible. Leaders and supervisors learned to listen far better than they had ever listened before and that single factor is credited with changing the dynamics of behavior in their group.

Numerous people commented about the impact on their families through the application of simple Open Space principles.

One person talked about how the rowdiness and disrespect shown at the dinner table of a six-member family shifted to such a degree that the children and parents stayed at the table talking with each other, on a typical evening, long after the meal was finished. Another person reflected on how it completely changed her relationship with her teenage son who was demonstrating all the signs of becoming a delinquent. Another man spoke of how a group of his "old European cronies" who met every week to drink beer and smoke cigars had really never listened to each other. One night, in frustration, he slammed his beer can in the middle of the table and said, "No one's listening to each other here. Only he who has the beer can is allowed to speak." This single, simple intervention, modeled after the Talking Stick Ceremony, a creation of native Americans and regularly used in Open Space, is credited with changing the entire level of interaction among these old friends. By this person's testimony, "We now listen to each other and care for each other at levels far deeper and more intense than we have ever done, and we have known each other for most of our lives."

      Most of us would like to achieve these kind of changes while training and doing organizational development (OD) and see, immediately, the long-term ramifications of our work. What is inherent in the structure of the training that inhibits these changes? The answer is not clear, but there is obviously something in the process of Open Space that enhances learning far beyond most of our philosophies or structured exercises. In that process the participant is empowered to become the expert. In training and OD, we also want the expertise to lie with the participant, but they look to the trainer or consultant for direction. I submit that the traditional models for training and education undermine integrity and self-esteem.

I have come to understand that, with all my expertise developed over the years, and in the increasingly powerful ways I have learned to work with teams and organizations, the techniques I have learned to use so well may, in fact, be a major piece of the limitation in individual and organizational change. Serious review of our fundamental assumptions in training and OD seem appropriate if we are to approach our clients and organizations with a high level of integrity. Substantial risk-taking is obviously required because we may be able to do far more in a shorter period of time, and therefore, our jobs as OD trainers may not be as secure.

So What Have We Learned?

➤ Defining the problems to be addressed in the Open Space process with great clarity is much more difficult when an organization is in transition. Some problems that were defined were too small and innocuous and others which appeared to offer great opportunity were too large for the group to get its arms around.

➤ Senior management must be carefully evaluated to determine if they are really committed to these fundamental changes. Fear runs rampant in any transition when individual jobs are being restructured, let alone eliminated. Perhaps these changes can only be made through experiencing the process, but prior discussion with senior management about a commitment to the Open Space process would legitimatize future discussion. After-the-fact discussion may result in significant defensiveness.

➤ Because fear and uncertainty run high during organizational transitions, it became necessary to reconvene the group after lunch for a brief time to address any new concerns or add new topics to the market place bulletin board.

➤ It was helpful to float from session to session to keep a pulse on what was happening within the groups. The Open Space facilitator's presence, on numerous occasions, overcame the group fear of authority and allowed questions and discussions that resulted in significant alterations of the group's behavior and subsequent success in working on the defined problem.

➤ Some groups had trouble defining their actual job roles even several months into the reorganization, and were afraid to act with empowerment. The personalities of these people, and of management may not offer the potential for strong movement in some groups.

➤ Targeting the right people to attend Open Space sessions may be very difficult on a plant-wide basis. Open invitations may not be accepted if the political climate is unsupportive. On at least one occasion sufficient expertise was not present to address the group problem. Neither management nor the consultant understood the level of sophistication necessary to address the problem prior to the Open Space session.

➤ While Open Space "mentality" as opposed to the Open Space "technology" is emphasized when discussing the transition from the Open Space session back to the organization, most people never made this transition. One of the difficulties was that the group continued to see Open Space as a training program that should be directly transferable back to the plant. While this is true on occasion, it is seldom a way to run your organization on a daily basis. However, Open Space mentality is extremely beneficial when operating within a team-based structure.

➤ The honesty and clarity necessary to evaluate the success or benefits of Open Space is beneficial. While any single problem utilizing Open Space technology would provide most if not all the criteria for evaluation, something occurs within organizational transition that makes it difficult to assess what really happened. In this particular organization they thought typically in terms of measurable results. The plant was run by engineers and accountants. They often failed to see the movement which had occurred both at an individual and collective group level relative to learning to work together. They expected absolute, concrete results. While these did occur, sometimes they did so at a slower level than many would have liked. One Open Space session produced an incredible increase in awareness about the assumption of personal responsibility. The plant manager saw things he had never understood before; individuals became clear about the difference between making suggestions and taking the responsibility to make something happen. The whole group experienced a surge of energy around commitment to this transition at a low-energy point late on a Friday afternoon, and the spirit rose. While much progress was made with many small details of a problem, which in hindsight was too big to tackle in one day, many people later described this session as unsuccessful despite the fact that one small group found a way to save $435,000; and the whole group defined ways to save a total of over $750,000. Working with a mentality that says that was an unsuccessful day is still baffling.

➤ Specific strategies should, at a minimum, provide a forum for management to talk collectively and directly about their expectations and frustrations, as well as their excitement about the individuals and teams making a transition through Open Space.

➤ Follow through is critical, especially when Open Space is used as a transition mechanism. Humans tend to revert to old behavior patterns and extra effort is required to ensure that the transition holds.

For further information:
Hugh Huntington
P.O. Box 2379
Taos, New Mexico 87571
Telephone 505-776-8347

Chapter XI

Lessons from Open Space at the World Bank

Giles and Robbins Hopkins

Giles and Robbins Hopkins are husband and wife who share a consulting practice, but who almost never get to work together, even though they have both spent the last 15 years working with many of the same clients in education, healthcare, and international development. Despite the apparent separation, they are a team and learn from each other. Robbins is the trailblazer and exudes enthusiasm, Giles, the greybeard, prefers a low profile. Both of them are passionate about Open Space and take great satisfaction in giving it away in places others wouldn't try. The story of how they are doing all that in the World Bank follows.

One hundred people are sitting in a large circle taking stock of the first day of a 3-day strategic learning retreat for their organization. One of the senior managers receives the hand-held microphone from the person next to him as it makes its way around the circle, signaling the opportunity to comment. There is some anticipation as he stands since he is a well-known, albeit good-humored, skeptic. He says that when he heard that the retreat was going to use this new approach called Open Space, he was sure it would not work, certainly not in a place like the World Bank.

After the first day he is amazed at what is happening and is drawn to the obvious logic and simplicity of Open Space. In fact, he says, "I am going to pay this process the ultimate compliment, I am going to steal it immediately and use it the next chance I have."

That was the first strategic learning event that we designed and facilitated using Open Space Technology. Since that first experience in 1992, we have organized more than 30 strategic learning events for the World Bank using Open Space. Most of these have been "intact" work groups embarking on efforts to improve their own capacity to achieve their missions. Increasingly, these events include stakeholders from outside the sponsoring group on issues of broad concern in the development community. Although we are using Open Space with other clients, the scope of our experience with the World Bank has been a rich source of learning about how and why Open Space works. We are, therefore, taking this opportunity to recount some of those learnings in a "tale from Open Space."

The story begins several years ago when our small consulting practice was hunting for a design for a large strategic learning event – a retreat for 100 World Bank staff in one department. We had been facilitating retreats for clients in the international development world for many years. We were increasingly dissatisfied with the results even though the clients were happy with the events. We had stretched the facilitator's "bag of tricks" to the limit and felt we had reached a plateau in our own effectiveness. We were searching for a process that would:

➤ Be more consistent with the values we shared with our best clients in the international development sector, particularly a high value on empowering the clients to define their own needs and to evaluate the best processes for taking action.

➤ Short-circuit what we called the "arm-chair critic" syndrome. A planning committee invests long hours designing a retreat based on interviews of staff about their concerns and preferred agenda. Once the retreat begins some staff still do not feel invested in the agenda and are prone to sitting back and taking "pot shots." These were the "arm-chair critics," using their analytical skills with a negative impact.

➤ Energize large groups (100+) in ways that would produce internalized commitment to the developed objectives and actions by getting everyone fully and actively engaged, and to encourage leadership to emerge.

➤ Place us as consultants in a "right relationship" with our clients, allowing and even encouraging us to work from our most basic values and fundamental faith in human potential.

As is often the case when you are searching, a series of apparent coincidences led us to an answer – Open Space. With initial encouragement and guidance from Harrison Owen and a copy of *Riding the Tiger* in hand, we set off for Airlie House in Virginia with 100 World Bank staff for 2 days. We knew we were on the right track when one manager from the group arrived late in the morning as we were finishing our introductory large group session for the Open Space event. He came up to us and asked what was going on. I replied that we were well into the Open Space process. He said that he could feel the energy level upon walking into the room – it had "bowled him over" – and that something really exciting must be happening.

Though we were comfortable with the principles of the method, we were still unprepared for how quickly the group actually took responsibility. Usually a group this large required at least two facilitators, but by the afternoon of the first day, it was obvious that one of us could easily handle the remainder of the process. Giles went home to take care of the kids and came back at the end of the conference to pick up Robbins and attend the closing picnic. This was our first learning: one experienced facilitator familiar with and committed to the principles of Open Space is enough even for a hundred people or more. Since then we have also learned...

The Anxiety Litmus Test

Open Space scares people. It probably should. After all we are talking about creating a level playing field in which anyone present can convene a session and anyone can move from session to session. Obviously people with a high need to control process and outcomes are going to be anxious even contemplating such an approach. We have learned that a client's initial anxiety is a good litmus test. It means that they are trying to come to terms with the implications of placing so much faith in a group of staff and a process which sounds right, but is scary just the same.

Sharing Our Confidence

Our confidence in Open Space is based on experience but also on our basic faith that given the right environment, people will reach past their traditional dysfunctional meeting behaviors, and share their passion and creativity in a responsible way. As we move through the planning stages, one thing we do is re-explain the underlying values and principles of Open Space in ways that build the sponsoring group's confidence by helping them see how Open Space can be an expression of their values. For example, since the World Bank is heavily populated by economists, we explain the process in terms of a free market of buyers and sellers and a marketplace of ideas. Putting it in a familiar framework helps, but eventually there comes a time, usually right before the event, when we get a phone call from one of planning committee or the lead manager saying, "I'm really concerned this is going to bomb, that no one is going to stand up and offer a session. Tell me it is going work!" And we tell them. And it does. Thirty times (the number keeps growing) we have done this and every time it works. It works because given a chance, people want to make a difference.

Bigger is Actually Better

Most clients are starting from the assumption that if they want to accomplish anything they had better keep the number of participants manageable. Since they are working from a model of manageability, which assumes a high degree of control, they often are struggling with who not to invite. We come in with Open Space and say, "the more the merrier, let's get everybody in the room who needs to be there, your staff, your clients, your supervisors." This opens up entirely new possibilities for a retreat or learning event. The limitations now are driven by budget. Since dollar for dollar Open Space is a bargain compared to other conference methods, our clients are doing bigger and better things. This has meant more inclusion. For example, support staff are now always a part of Open Space retreats for intact groups we work with; they report that for the first time they feel they can fully participate, adding value and learning a lot. Bigger groups have also made it possible to "get the client in the room" and to bring in development practitioners from other organizations.

Convergence and Emergent Leadership

Our experience certainly validates Harrison Owen's rule of thumb that with one day you get a good discussion of the issues; with 2 days you get a good discussion of the issues and a good record of what was discussed with some recommendations; with 3 days you get all that plus some convergence around priority actions. We have evolved a method for follow-up which recognizes the emergent leadership and keeps those with a stake in the implementation clearly in the driver's seat of the follow-up process. Intact work groups often request assistance in implementing the recommendations from the event. We take part of the third day of the Open Space event or arrange for a half-day meeting after the participants return to their work place to begin that process.

    The first step in the implementation process requires priority setting and planning. We hold a follow-up meeting with the staff who convened sessions to finalize the session recommendations from which the large group will select priorities for action and will allocate resources. The session conveners help each other clarify their session recommendations and classify the sessions. Some of the sessions have no actionable recommendations as they were "discussion only" sessions and these are not included in the package of recommendations to be voted on. Other issues raised in the Open Space may already be under consideration in some fashion by standing committees or task forces and these are also removed from the larger set of sessions to the extent the group feels they are being handled. Some sessions have similar themes and may be combined by leaders to provide a single topic focus while still retaining the different sets of recommendations. Finally, some of the recommendations are too vague for others to understand and these may be rewritten with the suggestions of other group leaders and after consultation with the original session members. The final set of session summaries and recommendations is completed and distributed to all participants.

Once everyone has had a chance to review the recommendations, a full-group priority-setting session is convened. If the large-group priority-setting session is to be held as part of the Open Space event, the meeting of conveners can be held on the evening before the last day. If the full group is small, under 50, the session summaries and recommendations can be cleaned up in a full-group session and the priority-setting session can be done with the entire group immediately afterwards.

The logistics of the "voting" are simple and consistent with the rest of Open Space. After the session packet is finalized, each person is given an agreed upon number of colored self-sticking dots with which to indicate his/her priority preferences for action. Typically for a group of 120, five colored dots are given to each person for voting. Each session summary with its recommendations is posted on the wall and people stick their dots on the summaries which represent for them either issues or recommendations that the group should regard as top priorities. The dots are tallied and the large group determines with the facilitator what will be addressed, by whom, in what time frame, and with what links to the formal management process of the group.

Further follow-up by us is negotiated as requested and may include a 6 month review meeting, support with specific groups on their terms of reference, clarification of objectives for the groups, etc. However, the pace of the group's progress and what is ultimately achieved remains the responsibility of the session conveners (now the emergent leadership) and the group members.

Maintaining the Integrity of the Process

In the spirit that Harrison has modeled, we make no claims of ownership of Open Space and encourage clients to use it where it may be valuable. One World Bank agricultural specialist sent us an email from Africa a week after an Open Space retreat for his division reporting that he had used the method successfully with a simultaneous translator for a country portfolio review meeting. His grasp of the underlying values of Open Space was critical, but many staff at the World Bank have been experimenting with more participatory approaches to development work and we increasingly get calls for advice on designing more participatory processes, and staff run Open Space events. We now think about our work as temporarily uncovering Open Space and holding it open for those who can benefit from the experience. In this sense Open Space is like another time/space dimension that is always there, but requires an act of faith in order to cross over (the faith in people we mentioned earlier). This is not a faith that everyone shares, often for good and compelling reasons which are not part of our own experience.

Although the method is available to learn, few other consultants who work with the World Bank make much use of it, and even clients who have both the faith and competence to access it still often ask us to provide the facilitation year after year. This has led us to recognize the deep connection we have to Open Space and to take extreme care in the way we bring others into this different dimension. As a consequence, we find ourselves often saying, "No, Open Space is not what you want, it sounds as though you want a process where such and such happens; let me recommend someone who would be good at facilitating that for you." This is not really a question of being a purist about process, but being clear about what kind of relationship we want to have to the people we work with and how to get it. If the client is tightly attached to a narrow vision of a particular outcome for an event, we take that as a red warning flag. It may be a valid goal; it's just not a good place for us to help.

Once You Have Been There, It Just Keeps Getting Better

It is quite common for participants to be skeptical at the outset, but somehow once they get into Open Space they find they know what they are doing. One group Robbins worked with held two Open Space events within six months of each other. The two differed in that the first one had two additional "mandatory" full-group sessions (in case the Open Space was a bomb) before the Open Space began. At their second conference they got right into the Open Space without "warm-up" sessions. The sessions at the second conference were qualitatively different in that they were more focused, substantive, and future-oriented as indicated by the summaries and the comments in the plenary session. The staff at the second conference commented that they came expecting to accomplish needed tasks, and they did.

Other differences emerge with repeater groups. There is often more lobbying to get certain people to particular sessions and the sessions are usually smaller because staff are less prone to combine similar topics into a large session. Also, if a large session evolves, leaders are likely to suggest that the session be broken into smaller groups so that participants can have more air time to discuss the issues.

Leaders take more interest in publicizing their topics the second time around and some even develop posters for the halls to entice others to come. The titles of the sessions become more provocative with repeater groups. And the repeater groups report that they focus on specific strategies and recommendations during the first day rather than building up to these during the second day as usually happens for a first time Open Space group.

Several participants in different Open Space events have commented that once the opening session was finished, everyone just seemed to be able to do whatever was needed to have a useful experience. The ability of groups to self-manage with a minimum of facilitator intervention continually amazes participants and seems to grow with each successive Open Space event.

Whose Success is This Anyway?

The most gratifying feeling about doing Open Space over the past few years at the World Bank has been to share in people's joy and energy as they realize how much they have accomplished and what a good time they have had doing it. They are living from their best selves, and the amount of positive reinforcement that flows is stunning. The contrast is stark because most staff report that the culture of cynicism is rampant in the institution.

One of the best feelings in the world for us is to tell our clients at the end of an event what a great job they have done and to know that we feel very little need for validation ourselves because we have been privileged to witness the passion and the responsibility of a hundred people doing what they were afraid they could not.

Is Open Space Better?

For those seeking an objective evaluation of Open Space before they experience it, it would be nice to be able to prove causal links with organizational improvements. In our experience, many well planned organizational interventions based on careful analysis of structure, process, job design, etc., ultimately fail because there is no change in day to day behavior as staff interact. Open Space starts by changing peoples behavior, calling forth their passion and responsibility, their interpersonal skill and natural leadership. Frankly, the quality of the experience is so much better than the alternatives, we haven't felt the need for formal evaluation. Since most of our work is based on referral and our clients are happy to talk to others about using Open Space, we take that as proof enough. These are the kinds of anecdotal evaluations we have heard.

➤ On the morning of the second day at an Open Space event of over 100 participants, one person with whom I had had no prior contact, came up to me and said, "You know, I haven't heard the words, *can't, impossible,* or *no* during this entire event. For this group that is remarkable. Why do you suppose that is?" We got into a discussion about how Open Space invites the best in folks to come out, and how they are operating from positive energy because they are making decisions which are good for them and they are doing things they think need doing.

➤ Several weeks after an Open Space event participants completed an attitude survey about a number of work-related issues and experiences. The Open Space conference and the follow-up activities were the highest scored items on the questionnaire. From talking with staff, the key seemed to be that during the conference each person felt fully responsible for his or her experience. Most of the rest of the time, staff reported feeling that others ran their lives, set their deadlines, set up the standards for performance, and evaluated their efforts. The challenge this group articulated based on their Open Space experience was how to get a sense of individual responsibility and accountability to be daily experiences for staff.

➤ Often clients are interested in the bottom line, that is, the substantive aspects of their jobs. In one conversation with an Open Space conferee and division manager, I asked what was effective about this method of meeting as compared to others he had attended. He proceeded to relate that during several sessions the entire process of assigning and reviewing work of the division had been re-thought, including changed emphasis on specific projects, new concepts and expectations for teams, and more timely procedures agreed to for reviewing projects when extenuating circumstances make earlier decisions inappropriate.

In a Bank where the goal is to lend money, quality projects are the business of the institution. He said, "Before at a retreat like this, these issues would have never been raised, much less effectively addressed. More likely, I would have had to listen to everyone's problems with how we were operating and then go back to the office and try to solve them myself."

➤ In another conversation, an administrator for a large department commented that the follow-up activities to the event had surprised everybody. She said that most of the time they got little or no follow-through on things agreed to at a conference, but this time the commitments to set up groups and bring recommendations to the departmental management team were still coming through fully 7 months after the conference. She attributed the staying power to the fact that the session leaders cared about the work they had agreed to pursue and the management team was positioned to support their efforts rather than to carry out the follow-up activities themselves as in the past.

➤ And finally, one group went to the Open Space event and completely surprised themselves by coming up with an extensive strategy and outline of a paper for their new director who was joining them in a few days. This group used their third conference day to strategize, develop, and present a case stating how they saw their role and areas of expertise as meeting the regional priorities in the face of other perceptions. After the conference, the division chief stated that there would have been no other way they could have all participated so fully in the designing of their own future. The chief continued by saying that the staff were much closer and focused as a result of the Open Space experience, and felt that they had developed an excellent paper for their new director with ownership from all staff.

Thus, the stories continue to carry the message about Open Space. Perhaps one of the unidentified strengths of Open Space is that it allows people to create important stories as they connect with their passions and gives them a way to recreate those positive feelings and experiences through the retelling of their stories to others who have not yet experienced Open Space.

For further information:
Giles and Robbins Hopkins
8201 Wahly Drive
Bethesda, Maryland 20817
USA
Telephone 301-469-8003

Chapter XII

Opening Small Spaces

Larry Peterson

Larry Peterson belongs to the small intrepid band of Canadians who first discovered Open Space. As of this date, Larry has opened space all over Canada, and with this piece he experiments with small spaces. My position has always been that anything less than a full day is insufficient, so Larry's suggestion borders on the heretical. However, in the world of Open Space, there is a fundamental law which takes precedence over any and all dogma: If it works, Do it! And it works.

Introduction

What if you only have three hours? What if people are tired from information sharing that had to be done? Can you still use Open Space Technology? I have used it in these small spaces and limited times with real success. Open Space Technology is such a powerful approach to meetings that they can be productive and even inspired in very small spaces and time frames.

In my role as meeting facilitator, I have usually encouraged a planning group to maximize the time in Open Space when it was appropriate. Not all planning groups are willing to take that risk. As well, it is often necessary to have other meeting processes in order to create the conditions for a meaningful use of Open Space Technology. I find this to be especially true in not-for-profit organizations such as churches, social services agencies or government organizations. Smaller and not-for-profit organizations often do not initially have the willingness, resources, or time to engage in long Open Space events. Smaller and not-for-profit organizations usually include volunteers, especially at the governing board level. If they have a weekend workshop or retreat, information sharing is usually a critical component. Some decisions by the whole group are also often required by the end of a meeting.

In working with these groups, I have used "Open Space Technology" in smaller time spaces than I would have imagined useful or possible. "Opening the space" for participants to create and self-organize a portion of a larger agenda can lead to surprising breakthroughs, engagement, and commitment. I will give some examples.

Planning a Community Event

A broad organization with a focus on community economic development had held citywide 3 day events in past years. One of the critiques was the lack of participation in workshop meetings. After hearing of Open Space Technology, the leaders decided to guide their next 3 day event with the aid of this navigation tool. However, this story is not about the community event itself, but about one of the planning meetings.

The organization, through its mailing list, invited whoever wanted to come to an evening planning meeting for 2½ hours. Forty people came. About half of those who came had never been to a meeting of the organization before, and few had experienced Open Space Technology. We had brought some basic materials in case there was a desire to try Open Space, and we had extra meeting space available. I was willing to give it a try in that short a time, but I was skeptical.

In the first 15 minutes of the meeting, the organization's staff described the proposed event and generated some enthusiasm for it. The group was willing to become involved in planning, using Open Space. So, I proceeded to create and hold the time and space. The theme question was, "What are the issues and opportunities for planning the event for which you have a passion and are willing to take responsibility?" It was a very practical theme. I suggested "start times" for the discussions that were one-half hour apart. The Principles and Law of Open Space were invoked. They could decide when to start and when it was over if the one-half hour times did not fit their discussion.

The group self-organized in about 20 minutes, and went into its discussion groups. They posted topics such as event advertising, inviting key people, and computer networking. To my surprise, most discussions did last only 30 minutes. They were also quite productive. In the closing "go-around," people reported their enthusiasm for some creative ideas that had emerged. One group "found" $5,000 funding for a communications process, funding that had eluded them for some time. People new to the organization reported that they now felt part of it, that their interests were included, and that they could see a way to add their abilities. All of this in half-an-hour meeting times.

A number of the ideas and plans from this session were followed-up by ad-hoc groups or the organization's own leadership and staff. The brief planning meeting had made a real contribution. (For those who are interested, the 3 day event went moderately well. Using Open Space to create the agenda of a 3 day, non-residential, community event worked well for those who wanted to do things. Some new community economic ventures were created. It did not work as well for those who wanted to come and hear others present. However, that is a story for another time.)

A Small Governing Board

I have facilitated the annual retreat of the governing board of a small service organization for the last 3 years. It is a group of 15 people. The first two weekend events were participatory, but not in Open Space. The planning team and lead staff felt that some basic clarity of focus and direction were required, as well as a good understanding of the services that were being governed. Thus, I enabled and guided information-sharing, role-clarification, and direction-setting discussions and decisions. As the clarity and momentum developed the board realized that a portion of its program was not in keeping with its understanding of its mission.

It had developed the momentum to govern and took appropriate action. This had all happened without the use of Open Space Technology, even though the perspectives of organizational transformation and evoking spirit had informed the design of the weekend events.

At the last event of the weekend, the conditions were right for Open Space. A board meeting was needed to deal with a critical issue: there was new data about the services to be presented. Also, the executive staff had just become clear about the impact of the new legislation on their service. It was now apparent that some major aspects of their work would need to transform or be closed. They could not become an exception to the new legislation.

After the board meeting, and the presentation and clarification of critical information, there were only 3 hours left for Open Space. Again, surprising things happened in a short time. The theme was the "next year's work of the board." Topics were posted with regard to the major issues facing the organization. Board members went into small groups and tackled topics in 45-minute sessions. Some met outside and others used breakout rooms. In the closing 45 minutes they described the surprising amount of work they had accomplished. They directed some items to ongoing committees and new groups emerged for others. They also stated how surprised they were that this approach to meetings had engaged their energy just when they were reeling from the news of the impact of the new legislation.

A Large Governing Board

I also recently facilitated a meeting of the governing board of a national church organization. It had 40 participants including primates, bishops, archdeacons, church administrative leaders, and church staff. It is a structurally complicated organization with some serious organizational problems. The Open Space portion of the agenda was planned for the last evening and part of the following morning of a 3 day event. It was not supposed to be a major portion of the meeting. This governing board had recently been appointed for a new term and the planning committee assumed it needed to better understand the organization and context. Thus, there was a lot of input and clarifying discussion. By the time we got to the Open Space, a financial, staffing, and organizational crisis had become apparent. It was beyond most people's expectations.

The initiation of Open Space had been planned for one of the worst times of the day, right before dinner. People had been listening all afternoon to increasingly discouraging data; and they were tired. The theme was "the issues and opportunities for the next year of the governing board." Not many topics were put up, as people were truly tired. However, unlike the previous two examples, we did have time for four one-hour sessions and it was overnight.

Open Space groups were to either initiate action or develop proposals to come to the governing board late the next morning. Decisions had to be made about staffing and funding for the next year. The leaders were somewhat anxious about opening the space when the time seemed so precious and some decisions were required at this meeting.

Again, I was surprised that it worked so well. When the participants created the agenda and began to self-manage it, some of their energy came back. The discussions were often exciting and productive. Proposals that had come from committees were reworked. New images of the future of the organization were explored. Practical steps for working together were developed. Some critical staffing accountability issues were explored from a variety of perspectives. There was enough time in Open Space for discussions to build on one another and for "bumblebees" to do their work. Substantial consensus on how to approach the critical issues did emerge in the Open Space.

After Open Space Technology was closed, the governing board moved into a decision-making meeting. The decisions were based on previous committee work and on proposals coming out of Open Space. Decisions went much faster than anticipated. Proposals were phrased in ways that would gain consensus, with only limited modification. People were tired upon leaving, but there was a positive Spirit and a sense of momentum on the critical issues.

Reflections

Thus, my experience is that Open Space can be a powerful approach to meetings, even in small time frames. If the theme is clear and the commitment present, then opening a space for 2 to 3 hours can be productive in a smaller group. I do not think it would work well for groups over 50 participants in a very short time frame, unless they know the process well. I could be wrong.

Open Space Technology is a meeting technique that works. However, it is much more than that. It embodies a new awareness of how best to organize for productive work. It demonstrates that *self-organization* can be more effective and inspired than imposed-organization. With this perspective, the technique can be appropriately stretched and molded to the situation and the people. Without this perspective however, I think Open Space becomes just another process to form work groups – losing its potential.

I also think that organizations are increasingly conscious that they live in Open Space most of the time. Given the pace of change, they are constantly between letting go of what used to work and finding what will work next. Opening larger spaces for self-organizing and spirit will be required of effective organizations and leadership. This will not just happen at special events, but in the ongoing flow of the organization's work. Opening small spaces is part of that process.

For further information:
Larry Peterson
41 Appleton Ave.
Toronto, ONT M6E 3A4
CANADA
Telephone 416-653-4829

Chapter XIII

A Letter from South Africa

Barry Lessing

The use of Open Space internationally is growing, particularly in areas of high stress and conflict. South Africa is certainly a leader in both those areas, and the following letter from Barry Lessing gives something of the flavor of a first time experience. What Barry does not describe is his second time out. On that occasion he assembled the 300 senior executives who manage the dozen or so companies under his care. Apparently they had never all met before, and many were strangers to each other. According to all reports, the affair was an outstanding success, laying the ground work for cooperative activities in a most confusing environment.

Dear Harrison,

My name is Barry Lessing, and I am the Deputy Managing Director of Transnet, the national transport company of South Africa which is (for lack of a better description) responsible for the national railways, South African Airways, South African harbours, the network of petroleum pipelines, and a road transport division.

I met you some time ago in Johannesburg when you gave a full-day course on Open Space. My gut reaction at the time was that this technique sounds and feels right, and that it will work because there actually are no forces pulling it in any other direction. From that point on I was looking for a way to use it so that I could have some firsthand experience with it.

During the weekend of 13-15 August I called together a conference on the unlikely topic (for a company like Transnet) of *Issues and Opportunities for Choirs and Choir Music in a New South Africa.* The reason is that Transnet is actually involved in establishing itself as a company involved in all sorts of community issues, and it has become very involved in musical events of different kinds, of which choral music is a specific example.

So, 6 weeks before the time we started arranging the conference. Fortunately we have a magnificent venue in the form of our training college at Esselen Park near Johannesburg where we had a big hall plus all other facilities, including residential, computer, and publishing facilities. In the end we attracted about 80 people from all over the country, of which about 55 were black and 25 were white.

I am writing this letter to you to thank you for introducing me to the concept of Open Space Technology. I bravely and ignorantly decided to use myself as the facilitator, so I was careful to follow your guidelines as scrupulously as possible, since I had no practical experience of my own. Two comments at this stage: (1) I took only 20 minutes to introduce the topic and explain the process (of which I am very proud); and (2) without exception, at the end of the 20 minutes, the observers whom I invited were convinced that they were attending my funeral service (which is interesting). Even the people who helped me to organise it, and knew (second hand from me) about the principles involved, had serious doubts about the process. I must say I didn't know about their disbelief at the time, but even if I did I suppose it would not have affected my own unshakeable faith in what I *knew* was going to happen.

The results were excellent (50-page book 48 hours later, great depth of discussion) but the most important thing in my opinion was the dynamics which took place in the group: the mix of creativity and energy which was released; the welding of interests; and the discovery of unexpected knowledge and insight across cultural borders. This was an experience which was a first for many of them.

I have also come to the conclusion that you are very wise, and probably pretty safe to make the technology available to everybody without charging "royalties" of some kind, because I believe that few people would naturally be able to fulfill the role of facilitator, and even less will be interested enough to do so for themselves.

So this letter is simply to thank you for introducing me to the concept, for the clear notes you gave with your lecture, and for the excellent handbook which I found *Open Space Technology* to be. The possible applications for this technology in South Africa at the present time is almost unlimited.

Thanks once again for a brilliantly conceived process which you have beautifully refined into something simple and direct and workable!

Barry Lessing

Chapter XIV

Eur-Open Space II

Roger Benson

Roger Benson is a European consultant. Exactly when and how he first ran into Open Space I do not know, but for several years we have corresponded, and in the fall of 1994, Roger took the plunge. The conventional wisdom is sure that Open Space in a European environment is questionable, if not doomed to failure. While there are certainly cultural differences, it turns out that Open Space works on the Continent as it does on other parts of the planet. At least that is Roger's story.

Regarding my experience ... We recently ran a 6-day conference/course for all (140) of the leadership trainers for L M Ericsson worldwide. As part of the design I suggested that a minimum of 2 days be spent in pure Open Space where they could learn from one another's accumulated wisdom. No one on the design team had experience of such a format, and needless to say, they were very uncomfortable. At the same time, they knew it was the right thing to do ... so we did. We have yet to receive the evaluations, but from the closing feedback it seems the end result was very good, with only a few wanting more structure in the name of "efficiency" (read: less internal tension).

The event was held at Corpus Christi College in Oxford; and we had the place to ourselves. The first part of the conference consisted of 2½ days in typical conference format. The content was a mixture of offerings to (a) meet the common needs of the entire group as determined by their feedback prior to the event (such as Ericsson's overall strategy, reviewing the common forces impacting their training, and development functions in the various companies, etc.); and (b) offer something new for them to experience for possible inclusion in their own trainings; and c) to build this entire group as an international network. Included were some simple outdoor "leadership challenge" exercises and concluding with a boat trip up and down the local river, punting to the pub and back.

The next 2 days were conducted in classic Open Space style, following your described format quite closely to give them a rather pure experience that they could modify as necessary in the future. The first day was completely theirs. The second had several pre-scheduled workshops and/or resource presenters, along with the open choices.   At the start of the day, I gave the participants a very clear "double message": *"These pre-scheduled sessions are good and could not be arranged for earlier ... and ... do what you really want to since the responsibility is yours to get what you want from this time."* This went reasonably well except for a fairly high load of guilt felt by participants since few attended some of the pre-planned sessions. I completely agree that nothing should be pre-scheduled in Open Space.

The last half day was scheduled for completion, next steps, etc., during which we again took the lead to set-up an exercise. I was a bit concerned at trying to take back the organising responsibility here, but again it went OK. I think this was largely due to the topic: *How do we continue after this event as a working and useful network?*

That was the set-up. The result: Participants very much liked taking responsibility for their own development. And they very much liked learning and sharing with each other. As trainers they are all used to being firmly in control, so the transition from highly structured presenter-centered to limited structure, participant-centered was very abrupt and for some a bit shocking.

All of the predictable dynamics of our previous experiences with Open Space occurred, but perhaps a bit earlier. People tried to get me to do some additional organising of the presentations on the bulletin board as more and more were posted (and their internal tension increased). When the last presentation was announced I tried to get everyone to just sit still and look over the results for a few seconds before jumping into action at the opening of the Market Place. But no way !!! Several simultaneous competing suggestions as to how to organise the postings better drowned me out and one participant said, "Hey, we're in control now. Just stand back." So I did, and left the tent. When I returned in 10 minutes or so, the market was swarming and the first session was beginning. Again a couple of people suggested that things should be organised a bit better; I said, "Good idea, why don't you do it?" Not what they expected or wanted to hear. By that evening, someone had re-organised the board into session areas – all session 1 topics here, session 2 there, session 3 next, etc. This indeed was a clearer arrangement to help participants to organise their own agendas, and one which I could easily have done ... and may do next time. But I can see that it pre-defines thinking into just the "sessions" format and I did not want that. I wanted them to look at break times, lunch, topics that span multiple sessions, etc. But in retrospect, it would have eased some of the anxiety.

To organize sessions I used a room/time matrix with *Post-It* notes and it worked very well. Many here in Europe seem to like to use the technology for purely a process experience – gather everyone in the room, say "Hi," and that's it. I am not interested in that at all as this design seldom suits the real task at hand! I much prefer providing the skeleton and letting participants flesh it out rather than provide nothing at all, and it has worked quite well.

So all in all, we successfully incorporated a full Open Space session inside a more highly structured conference. I did a lot of verbal positioning to ease the transition and bring participants along as easily as possible. One of these is the use of group agreements/guidelines that I always use in my events. This time I used the following:

- Punctuality
- Confidentiality
- Listening – one meeting at a time.
- Statements – taking personal responsibility.
- Honesty
- Openness
- Respect – for differences, for each other, for "the space."
- Have some FUN!!

I emphasised and reinforced the theme of self-responsibility throughout the first 2 days, as well as the amount of wisdom and experience in the room waiting to be shared. So they were ready to share when the Open Space began. I also found it useful in this case to structure the evening news slightly to help deepen the time. I divided it between Announcements and Sharing (of experience), primarily to encourage real sharing. This went OK. And for the final closing, we had the same, followed by a clear question-and-answer debriefing of the technology itself so they could further discuss using Open Space in their home organizations. I emphasized when it should and should not be used, and because they were all trainers, the bit about needing to let go control. The last item was certainly the source of the most internal conflicts. The hardest part to get across is the role of the organiser/facilitator regarding holding a clear space, awareness of the energy levels, etc. This is simply a higher dimension than most had ever considered and is not easily covered in 5 minutes. But I think it vitally important, a very developmental step in itself for the individuals involved.

So all in all, Open Space has been successfully introduced into Ericsson, and will no doubt be tried by some of these trainers. I also hope to propose several larger events for a different purpose next year. The chance of their being accepted is quite low, but it is what they need in the particular areas in which I am working. Time will tell.

For further information:
Roger Benson
Creative Partnerships
Fiskaruddsvagen 63
144 62 Ronninge SWEDEN
Telephone 46-8-532-50820

Chapter XV

Open Space in the Antioch Graduate Management Program

Jan Gray

Ever since Open Space happened it has been more than apparent that learning at superior levels takes place in this environment. The hows and whys remain to be ferreted out, but every moment seems to become a learning moment. Given our normal propensity to equate learning with quiet and order, this state of affairs comes as something of a surprise. The people at the Antioch Graduate Management Program have taken the learning potential of Open Space very seriously, and Jan Gray has pulled together the comments and thoughts relative to this ground breaking effort.

Antioch University Seattle initiated its graduate management program in September 1992. Among faculty, design committee, and the first student cohort,[*] about a half-dozen learners had exposure to Open Space ranging from a brief introduction to several years of experience in facilitation.

Towards the end of the first year of the program, I was asked to form teams and organize "Student Designed Modules" for

---

[*] This is Antioch-speak for "class."

the second-year curriculum. The concept was a difficult one and after much effort and a great deal of complaining, a student suggested using the "Market Place" portion of Open Space to facilitate decision and commitment to module design concepts. As a result, the impossible became fact. Modules were selected, teams were formed, and the creative process got a "modified" Open Space kick-start.

The success of the students piqued the interest of others in learning about and doing more in Open Space. Several students took part in Harrison Owen's "Open Space Training" in early 1994. Meanwhile, the second cohort was also being introduced to Open Space. In April, the first cohort chose Open Space as a module format. Arrangements were made for students who did not wish to participate, but, in the end, participation was 100% except for one student waylaid by illness. The module was the foundation for development of an Antioch Seattle Management Institute.

By June, faculty members were ruminating about whether and how the entire program might be conducted in Open Space and Stephen Mercer, a member of the second graduate management cohort, had begun the following dialogue (used with permission) on the program's computer network...

An Open Space Conversation

Stephen H. Mercer: Greetings to my distinguished GMP associates. I'd like your help with an issue (and I'd especially like to capture the viewpoints of those finishing their second year of the program). The question is – what is, in your thinking, the value of "Open Space?" What are its strengths and weaknesses? We've been using Open Space in a number of GMP applications and some have participated beyond the program. But, as Cathy Puma said (tongue in cheek), "Open Space may not be the answer for EVERYTHING..." What IS it the answer for, and why?

Jenell DeMatteo: My most recent experience with Open Space was trying to tackle a specific agenda item for an organization. In my case – how to re-structure the organization. My perspective is that for Open Space, that topic was too specific. Instead though, we found a number of hot topics that are facing the organization. I think this is very useful and works well with an open format. In a sense, it was a way to tap into the heartbeat of the people in the organization. What are the issues, concerns, prospects for the future? This, I believe, is very powerful.

Stephen H. Mercer: Thanks for the observation, Jenell ... a way to tap into the heartbeat of the people is an interesting perspective. Is it too spontaneous for tackling specific issues or for "problem-solving?" (By "spontaneous" I mean without prior preparation, such as research or planning).

Jan Gray: Hi Stephen. I'm conducting pretty specific Open Space meetings for the Seattle Waldorf school. The 12-month plan was the latest. It works both for the task at hand and for community building. Please see today's (Sunday, June 5, 1994) *New York Times* Business section pages, for the story of Rockport shoes.

Mary Anderson: Stephen: Thanks for initiating this item. And thanks, Jan, for citing the *New York Times* article. It gives a credible introduction to the inexperienced out there in the biz world. My take on Open Space is that it's a tool for things like
- Finding people's interests and energies.
- Finding ideas people are actually willing to work on.
- Discovering where real, but submerged, issues are.
- Developing approaches to solving problems.
- Solving problems in a synergistic way, if the knowledge about what needs to be done resides in a group.

Open Space discussions can draw out parts of the answer from several people, allowing the group to create or discover the whole answer together. Open Space is not project management, but would be a great set-up to launch a project – or a planning process. Open Space can set the purpose, commitment, and project or process design. Follow-through tasks, including research, happen afterward; subsequent decisions to be made after more information is developed could be approached in the usual ways, or with another round of Open Space.

Stephen H. Mercer: Thank you, Jan and Mary. Your comments really help. Open Space has taken a measure of credibility in the world of business and can be useful as a tool to focus interest and commitment. Okay, but what makes Open Space more useful than what we used to call "rap sessions," or an informal evening over beers (or coffee)? And is it as effective in focusing energy and commitment as other methodologies, such as "Future Search Conferences"?

Julie R. Wadkins: RE: Open Space as compared to "rap sessions" (I think that term is before my time actually) or an informal evening. I think the most pronounced difference and credibility-building aspect is the *accountability* of Open Space. Our *modus operandi* for Open Space includes a harvest component in which we discuss how the different topics had meaning and/or how the Open Space topic fits in with our lives (work, home, whatever) – I have a sense that something will "happen" as a result of the Open Space. I don't necessarily get that sense with the informal evenings. What do others think?

Anne Morgan Stadler: Open Space has several distinctive qualities which "make it work." The two main ones are that people *take* responsibility, and follow what has heart and meaning for them. Therefore, you get work which is actually related to the manifestation of Spirit in the moment. It is "effective" in focusing energy because it offers a medium for energy to reveal itself. It is particularly effective because the diversity present in a group will surface – thus allowing the group to see itself whole, in real time, to experience its full potential. When I say manifestation of Spirit, I mean that Spirit (that indefinable essence) is realized by people or things acting or being tangible. Choosing to stand up for what you care about in regard to a particular topic or question is realizing Spirit/manifesting Spirit.

The theme or focal question provides focus – standing up for what has heart and meaning for you provides manifestation of Spirit in the moment. Writing down and circulating the learning and intentions expressed in Open Space provides ongoing learning for the community as a whole. To me, all these elements are fundamental to Open Space. They can all be applied in management of *any* activity an organization is doing.

I think, after doing Open Space for 5 years in various places, situations, organizational settings, etc., that Open Space is a way of being in community with people, period. It can be applied in meetings. It can be applied in management. It can be applied in personal discipline or practice. It is a superb support for manifesting diversity and living with the conflict of being in diversity. This network activity is Open Space and we are continually learning how to support that well. But if it works, it is Open Space on Open Space. Thanks for putting this item up. It's a great contribution to continuing learning about how to be/manifest a learning community!! You know, when I say it (Open Space) can be applied in those various realms (as I said earlier), what I mean is the principles of OS (whoever comes are the right people, whatever happens is the only thing that could have, whenever it starts is the right time, when its over its over *and* take responsibility for what has heart and meaning for you (the law of two feet). Those principles apply to management, organizational design, meeting together, being a person in a group, etc. If you add Angeles Arrien's fourfold way – show up, pay attention to what has heart and meaning, tell the truth, be open to outcomes – you see a match which constitutes a way for the individual to *be* in Open Space. Well.... thanks again.

Stephen H. Mercer: Thank you, Julie and Anne, for the thoughtful responses. More for us to chew on. Personally, I can see the accountability factor that Julie mentioned as being a distinction (although I wonder if it's not possible to have a similar measure of accountability as part of more informal dialogue settings). And I appreciate the clarification of the practice of Open Space, from Anne's perspective. My "aha" was, "You mean we can practice 'Open Space' in other ways?"

My only involvement with Open Space has been through the GMP. And as I read Anne's comment describing OS as "work that is... manifestation of Spirit in the moment" I realized I was near the center of my issue. Some are not spontaneous. Some of our cohorts need time to prepare comments and ideas to offer the community. How can OS accommodate everyone? And what about building in time for research as well as preparation? Would that not add significant value?

A critic of OS (as we practice it) might object that it is just another example of the Westerner's desire for instant gratification. If I understand Anne correctly, OS is a big enough concept to accommodate different expressions, including prep time. Does this mean that the manner in which we're approaching next year's student-directed modules (SDMs) could be classified as OS?

Jan Gray: Hi Stephen, I don't know how you planned your SDMs but ours included a bit of Open Space (not the whole thing, though). I am working on Open Space now in a very large organization and it is *abundantly clear* that proper prior planning is needed to achieve specific goals. There needs to be appropriate framing, support, and follow-through. I know Anne did quite a bit of research in preparation for her University of Chicago Open

Space. And as to instant gratification... well, not mine anyway. Peace.

Brad R. Falk: Steve, I think you can have different types of Open Space experiences. Some topics can be done spur of the moment, while others are more suited for indepth preparation by all participants.

Janice R. Greene: One of the things I found: trying to use Open Space in a class where attendance is required violates the principle of, "Whoever is there are the right people." When we do Open Space in a classroom situation, I think you benefit from the flexibility but I don't consider it real Open Space. The only 'real' Open Space that I've attended was in India. It was a wonderful, life-changing experience. (Not to say this happens all the time). I think the real secret of Open Space is being open to outcomes. What we tend to do in western society is fix the outcome then decide and complete the steps we need to reach it, with everyone marching in line. In Open Space I can choose only what I'm interested in and take charge of what I'm passionate about. There may be several different outcomes in relation to one topic with people who care enough about the outcomes to continue on and be involved. There is no reason for those who choose to prepare not to, but there's no reason to prepare for those who don't wish. It's Open Space.

Stephen H. Mercer: Thanks, Jan, Brad, and Janice. I'm getting a sense for how large and varied and "open" the Open Space methodology is. And I appreciate the amount of preparation that goes into the event. I'm fascinated by your comments, Janice, about how we violate the "right people" principle when participants are required to attend. I'm interested in hearing from you and other community members about experiences that illustrate the problem. Maybe my observation of different levels of participation is related more to this and less to behavior preferences (some are less spontaneous than others).

Christopher J. Carter: Great item, Stephen. It was hard to wait for all the previous responses to scroll by to get my two bits in. I agree with Janice about outcomes. The most surprising thing about Open Space for me is the variety of outcomes that are possible. Sure as shootin' the one time we as managers start to expect a certain outcome from OS, the group is really going to take us by surprise. My experience (limited to the GMP and some other experiences) with OS outcomes are *always* surprising, revealing, and improbable to imagine from any other methodology. That said, there is a place for more directed processes like Future Search. In fact, this summer, I'm participating in an Antioch Whole Systems study of Future Search. I think the two methods are complementary and compatible. At least, from what I know so far of Future Search. Harrison Owen himself said that if you can create another process that solves your organizational problem, try it before using Open Space. The point is: OS is not for everything but it can be used in more places than we might think. It's best with large numbers of people I think!

Anne Morgan Stadler: In a couple of instances, the University of Chicago Biological Sciences and the National Dairy Development Board (NDDB) in India, people are using Open Space principles for managing items which continue beyond the Open Space meeting or event. They're using email in Chicago, and when follow-up committees began their work they invited anyone who cared about the subject to participate. The initial committees decided to continue their work 'cause they couldn't finish in the time allotted for the initiating Open Space event. Then, they opened it for others who hadn't been part of the initial group to participate in the continuing work. At NDDB in India, they're using Open Space as a way of checking their process as they re-envision and regenerate the organization ... moving toward partnership. But these are Open Space events, held to allow people to contribute to the work of the core group/resource group which is guiding the whole process of organizational change.

I've always thought that one could adopt a method of deploying people – especially in design phase of a project – by asking for a certain number of volunteers from each stakeholder group you needed to involve (whoever comes are the right people), and giving them the design task and responsibility. In a way that's what the University of Chicago folks did. I haven't yet heard what the outcome has been – but for a while they were doing just fine maintaining the process and not sliding back into the usual power and role culture. That was the result of very explicit conversations between me and the two deans (who hired me) before the event itself took place, so that they were in clear agreement as to how the Open Space would serve them most effectively. Then, we debriefed afterwards, discussing how the continuing process and oversight of it could evolve. I'm really eager to continue to engage with these kinds of applications – and I know it's not easy, although the form and principles seem to match a flattened hierarchy, linked via email and computer networked databases, most efficiently.

Susan M. Mann: Chris – Re: Future Search Conference (FSC), I'm very interested in hearing more about what you're doing this summer. I attended a conference led by Marvin Weisbord and am now "certified" to lead an FSC. What you say is true – the OS process is highly compatible with the FSC process. In fact, Weisbord suggested a particular point in the FSC where he believes it fits in beautifully. Steve – this is an excellent topic, thanks for introducing it. Jan and Anne, your comments are helping me learn more about what OS is really about. I've gotten a lot out of the OS we've done in year one. It is clearly an approach that many of us structured banking and engineering types may feel "stretched" by at first. And that's part of why I believe it has value.

Stephen H. Mercer: Great activity here! We started with questions and concerns about Open Space and that has been a springboard to great feedback on both OS and other, related applications, such as Future Search. But I'm not sure we're hearing the whole story. Maybe I'm chasing something that's not there, but my sense is that not everyone is as enamored with our GMP OS experiences as our conversations, up to now, would have us believe. Janice raised the issue about voluntary participation (or lack of). I'd sure like to explore that further. And I think some of us just quietly go along with OS activities. Does it not work for everyone? If that's the case, why not?

Ron Thomas: This is a great conversation on Open Space. We need to send Harrison a copy. As some of you know I've just returned from facilitating a process at Independence Hall for the National Park Service – you know, the birth place of modern democracy and all that. The process was to engage the public in a dialogue on the future of Independence Hall Park. What worked? The Open Space qualities that empowered people to envision the future and share their ideas with the group. What didn't work? The professional Park Service people's perceived need to get specific information in a specific format for *their* needs. When they didn't get the answers on the first day they started to panic. The challenge was keeping them cool until the third day as the answers emerged. Open Space is a sure road to empowerment and from empowerment come ideas, energy, and *action*. People will do what they invent. The problem is the confidence of the gatekeepers.

Cathy Puma: Steve – Have you ever considered a career as a talk-show host? You have a great way of facilitating dialogue!! RE: Open Space: I had never heard of OS prior to the GMP. We tried it a couple of times the first year, but the OS experts in our class say in retrospect that what we did wasn't *really* Open Space, but rather a modified version of it. The fact that we didn't do it *exactly by the book* is irrelevant to me (but probably very relevant to others). What counted for me was the outcome – which I believe was successful for defining our student-designed modules. Still, I don't believe it's the elixir for everything – and of course, the organization's culture makes a big difference in determining whether it's a good facilitation tool.

Janice R. Greene: Cathy, what we did in the first year was use the parking lot idea; it was effective, but I've seen it be more effective when not billed as Open Space and used as a part of another method. The Institute of Cultural affairs for example, uses the same brainstorm concept with some follow-up by other organizing methods that I find more effective than partial Open Space. As for Open Space, it is my preferred method of organizing, bringing ideas to the table, finding what has energy for people, etc., not my preferred method of project planning though.

Stephen H. Mercer: Ron, it sounds like you had some tense moments at the National Park Service event. Why did the staff have difficulty being open to outcomes? Culture? Lack of understanding about the intent of OS? Were they otherwise unprepared for the event? Thanks for the insight. Cathy, your comment about the organization's culture making a big difference in determining the effectiveness of OS as a facilitation tool resonated with me. I wondered if that wasn't what Ron was dealing with at the National Park Service. (Thanks for the nice words). Janice, whenever you respond to this item I have a hundred follow-on questions I'd like to ask you. Here's one for you and the rest of the gang: If what we do is "partial" Open Space, what changes would we have to make in the GMP to make "full" OS possible?

Anne Morgan Stadler: One thing I feel about using "partial Open Space" is if you aren't clear about what are the minimum basic requirements, you can lose the energy of Open Space in an attempt at partial Open Space. One basic requirement is a theme question (framing the learning/work intention). Another basic requirement is taking responsibility for what you really care about – not brainstorming what anyone can do (or someone else can do) but standing up for your own participation.

Another basic requirement is being open to outcomes, and being open to whoever comes and whatever time it takes to do the task (that is: the planners need to enable a way for people to follow up on their interests – like this email, or like planning in advance what to do about using the feedback, and letting people know clearly what continuing process is going on or not going to go on). Organizing a meeting and then having an hour and half for Open Space (as happened at an ICOD conference I attended once) just doesn't allow for the generative and creative effects of Open Space to materialize. It feels creative, and is more effective than keeping people glued to a pre-planned schedule all the time, but it ain't IT.

What would we have to do? It would have to be a process that fits some basic intention of the program. Faculty and students would have to get adept at applying the basic principles in their daily work and meeting activities (for instance, suppose there's an opportunity for identifying what our learning community is? We generate ideas, continuing themes, they then continue via email and team work to contribute new learning and ideas into the program. People are invited to join conversations or working teams on the basis of what they truly care about, etc.). That happened most effectively in the Pod 2's choosing of issues to focus on in the second year. Did Pod 1 do Open Space for that also? What do you think? How would Open Space be useful on-going process and set of principles for either the program, or any learning organization??

Anne Morgan Stadler: Oh, I wanted to share a thought I had re: Open Space, Appreciative Inquiry, and some of the applications of Arny Mindell's conflict resolution group process stuff. You know David Bohm's idea about implicate order – that there are fundamental energy patterns which give rise to differentiated tangible biological entities and ecosystems (I hope that does justice to his fundamental idea) – well... I wonder if Open Space and Appreciative Inquiry (at least) reveal the implicate energy patterns and constellations of a group.

Open Space allows the emergence of "attractors" in the form of people who take responsibility etc... and it shows the patterns which may have been obscured by department structures, different boundaries (like customers, suppliers, competitors, etc.). The patterns are lively, alive, suffused with energy. They are implicit or secondary until Open Space allows the frame for opening up to them. Similarly with Appreciative Inquiry: you research what is lively, what is working, where the organization is operating at its highest potential. Then, you look at what is the pattern here? What can we learn about gaps which need filling, or things which need support and amplifying so that these patterns become the norm for the organization?

Anyhow... what do you think? Does that make sense to anyone else? Re: Mindell's group process stuff. The extent to which you can support full and congruent expression of the diversity of roles present in a group is the extent to which the group itself can move toward community/new consensus when it is in conflict. Again... you support the energetic expression of the underlying (not fully expressed) pattern. If you can do that, you are aligning with the "implicate temporal order" that is potentially available to the group. What do you think? I'm excited by this notion. I know it's abstract but it seems to me it may offer a fundamental analysis of why some interventions or management approaches could foster generative and learning communities with ease – and others don't cause they aren't harmonizing with the underlying energy patterns which give life. I'm really feeling wheeee... this is something I want to keep looking at.

Lots of love and thanks Steve for starting this. I'll tune in again in mid-July to see where you've all gone with the discussion. By the way, Susan from Hawaii, Marvin Weisbord, and Sandra Janoff were at the last November Open Space on Open Space. I'm happy to see that they're including it in part of their Future Search work. Hope you have good luck in getting the opportunity to "intern" with someone doing that. It's a good learning scheme: interning. Love.

Jeanine Britzmann: For all of the reasons already mentioned, I think that Open Space is a wonderful tool for certain situations or objectives. I'm considering using the method to create a conversation around the topic of "Teams" at Shurgard. We seem to get the request often in our organization to allow time in meetings for round table discussions and open format discussions so there doesn't seem to be a high need for structure – so OS might be very well accepted. I'll let ya know. The one thing that I have noticed kinda ties to Anne's thought on the energy fields, is that it takes a huge commitment and energy level put forth by the participants to make OS work. The last Open Space session we had during our module seemed tough to me because we were all acting a little weary and tired. See ya at the next exciting OS event.

Sally Fox: Perceptive Jeanine. I do think that what Anne is writing about, and what Open Space moves with is energy. I think that people can reclaim some of their authentic energy in longer periods of OS together. But that's harder to do in 3-4 hour bites when we are all tired.

Stephen H. Mercer: Thank you to everyone who contributed to this conversation. It has been (and could continue to be) a fascinating journey. I would still love to see ideas on ways we could better carry out the intent of OS in our GMP, and I'm interested in seeing how this topic evolves into others.

Mary Anderson: I am so impressed by the depth and breadth of this conversation. Thanks, Steve, for opening it up. This item is a valuable compendium of practical knowledge for OS users and pioneers. I bet Harrison Owen would be interested. Can someone send him a copy? As for my work world, the time is not quite right for OS, but I am laying groundwork by encouraging expanded decision-making spheres, strengthening the commitment/follow-through/results loop, and by bringing unnamed habits of "somebody ought to (or worse yet, "THEY ought to")" thinking out into the open. In Open Space, there ain't no THEY!

Gail Coopee: Mary, I will send Harrison a copy of our dialogue here. I think he will enjoy it. Thanks Steve, for starting this conversation. Anne, in response to your theory about Bohm and Mindell's underlying patterns – I think it is *very* interesting (some would say I like anything abstract!) and worth thinking some more about. I've been curious about the magic – and there definitely has been magic for me, in Open Space. I'll keep thinking about this and let you know what surfaces for me.

For further information contact:
Jan Gray
PO Box 30921
Seattle, Washington 98103-0921
USA
Telephone 206-789-4143

Chapter XVI

Safe Space

Suzanne Maxwell

Suzanne Maxwell lives in Placitas, New Mexico, some 20 miles from Albuquerque and very much in the middle of the desert. I think that may be important. If nothing else, she knows what natual Open Space is all about. That knowledge may also give her a special appreciation for the qualities of Open Space. Some spaces are mildly toxic, others assaultive to the senses, and a few downright dangerous. Productive Open Space is, to use Suzanne's words, "safe space."

A friend tells a story about taking her 20-year-old daughter to an Open Space event. After experiencing the Open Space process, her daughter commented, "These people are missing the point. This is not about Open Space, it's about *safe space*."

All my life I have not felt "safe" to be myself. In my past it seemed that when I was my deepest self in the context of other people, I often became the object of teasing, other people's seeming discomfort, and at times, outright ridicule. I have felt different from others most of my life, and rarely felt safe to show my true face. I have longed for the safety that welcomes my presence as long as I can remember.

Since we are a species that seems to want to make meaning for the events that befall us, a possible cancer diagnosis abounds with opportunities for self-examination. On this score at least, I am no different. In the pages that follow I do not present the presence of "safe space" as a cure for cancer or its absence as a cause. Rather, I have chosen to use the experience of cancer as a catapult for the personal learning that I probably should have done anyway. My question – "What is safe space, why is it important, and how do we talk about it?"

What is safe space?

Above all, the perception of being in *safe space* seems to begin within each of us as individuals, for example, a mindset that begins with me. I don't seem to be able to create safety outside myself unless I hold it to some degree already on the inside. Speaking from my own experience, I look back over my life and recall numerous events that seemed to say "the world is not safe," or "I can't be safe with these people, or this person, or in this place," or any one of a myriad of tiny hurts or perceived injustices that I (and I assume others) have collected from the moment of birth. Taken as a whole, these experiences have generated my view of the world and a whole set of protective behaviors designed to keep me safe, so that I might survive childhood, grow up, get married, have a career, raise a family, etc. Not a bad process.

The trouble is that in the flower of adulthood, this safety net developed in my childhood has proved to be inadequate to assist me in living life to its fullest expression. What I thought was *safe space* was in fact constricting, limiting, and controlling, a perimeter fence, designed to insulate me from perceived threats, not open me to life's potential. It has taken the experienced threat of a cancer in my left breast to move me out of the need for protection, and thrust me boldly into the rich, fragrant blossom of life at its fullest.

My breast cancer was diagnosed by half of the 25 or so pathologists who examined my tissue biopsy as *atypical cutis with hyperplasia* and by the other half as *carcinoma in situ*. In my terms, it meant half of them say I don't and half of them say I do. "Neither," my oncologist assured me, "You don't have cancer... it may never amount to anything," My surgeon said, "Even though you are having hot flashes, if you take any hormones whatsoever, with this type of condition, I guarantee you will have cancer." Clearly, in our medical model, the presence or absence of cancer can be a gray area. The confusion I felt between these seemingly opposing statements left me feeling like the *PushMePullYou* two-headed creature from an old Julie Andrews movie. "What am I supposed to do?!!" was the question that screamed through my whole being.

After living in overwhelmingly powerful angst of having no clear answers, and continuing to live thus, I have come to express the "what do I do" question in spiritual terms. Spiritually, what it means is that I get to choose. To live as though I do have cancer or to get closer to the conditions that may have contributed to its creation, work with what I find, and maybe live into not having it. For me the issue has become not how to beat cancer, but how to live life, how to show up fully as me. Dying, having lived fully, may be the highest form of healing.

So breast cancer has become my symbol and metaphor for living (after all, "What's a metaphor?"). What is the symbolic meaning of a female breast with cancer? To answer this question, it seems essential to have a sense of what a breast without cancer means. A woman's breast may feed and nourish, it is sensual and sexual and is central in the archetypal shape of womanhood. It is at its very essence feminine through and through. Being soft and round, it is perhaps symbolic of nurturance, reminiscent of circles that have no end, but are circles within circles, within circles. Open-ended and allowing ... safe space.

In our culture, breasts are valued as a symbol for sexual attraction. What little girl born in America aspires to grow up and have small, insignificant breasts. How would she ever attract a mate?! Ask any woman who has large ones though and she will tell you that they more often hang like albatrosses.

In corporate America, breasts, in my experience, have a different connotation. Their value as a source of food and nourishment is relegated to 90 days of mandatory parental "sick-leave." Their image of sensual sexuality is outlawed and considered inappropriate for the workplace. Thank goodness. Their symbolic interpretation of nurturance (and all that nurturing behaviors represent at work) is often seen as a sign of weakness, an irritating divergence from the task. Nurturance barely has a toehold on the corporate ladder that leads up to the glass ceiling.

The imagery evoked by a breast as soft and circular, or open-ended and allowing, seems to have no place in helping organizations reach their goals, increase their ROI, or expand their margins. Breasts in most places of business, in our current phase of history, literally or symbolically are essentially useless, to be avoided, and without value.

Realizing that I spend and have spent much of my waking life in corporate America, I felt shocked with the realization that so much of the essence of my being was not only not valued, it was to be avoided and repelled. I had somewhat learned to play the game and hide my true feelings and inner understandings in order to get by and be valued in the workplace. My most astounding insight was to become aware that if I lost my breasts, I would look more like a man (!) and symbolically be more well equipped to rise in the corporate world and shatter the glass ceiling. I was livid in my fury. Corporate America was most certainly not *safe space* for me.

I began to talk about my personal insight openly and with many people, curious about their experiences. In classrooms, client meetings, personal and professional groups, out of the woodwork came stories upon stories of women in executive or management positions who were leaving businesses or severely questioning their role in them after diagnoses of breast cancer or other potentially fatal diseases. Still others, with no life-threatening circumstances, reported that they felt as if they had to leave or "lose their soul." Some said, "I had to change my life or die." These stories came from women in organizations as small as sole proprietorships and as large as Fortune 100s. Men too, began to take me aside and whisper the dark truths of their own battles with cancer, heart disease, or severe injury and the questions their dances with death caused them to ask about the places they work and the way they operate within them. They spoke in hushed tones, in quiet corners, all the time looking furtively from side to side. In these hidden spaces they cried out their pain. They touched my heart. We cried together. How in the world have we created such unsafe spaces for people to live and work within.

The presence or absence of actual female breasts in business is not the issue I am tackling here (though it is a serious one); rather, the issue is the presence or absence of what they represent at a deeper symbolic level. Needing to make meaning of my own experience and use it to pave the way to work on my own issues that were in need of healing anyway, a potent question formulated in my mind. What essential parts of our beings as men and women are we asked to excise in order to climb high on the corporate ladder, and ultimately what is the terrible price organizations pay for their excision? How many of us on our deathbed, rise up and say, "I wish I had spent more time at work"?

Supported with this compelling question mark, I launched into an all-out search for rediscovering and recovering that which seemed so close to being cut out of my life ... the deeply feminine essence symbolized by my breasts. *Safe space.* When I use the words *feminine essence* I am not referring specifically to a gender issue, nor do I mean *female*. What *feminine essence* means to me in this context closely matches the feminine and masculine archetype descriptions that Carl Jung said exist in *every individual* man or woman. The feminine essence within each of us that balances our masculine. The yin and yang, soft and hard, logical and organic, the linear and the circular, thoughts and feelings, the dark and the light. I contend that both are absolutely essential elements of a fully functioning whole and that excluding one or the other creates a precarious and potentially lethal imbalance. Thus, our organizations, being linear, hard, built on logic, repellent of feelings, and full of the light of day are wildly out of balance. They are not safe spaces.

When I use these words, *safe space* or *safe spaces*, in public places, the hackles on the back of many people's neck stand up like the spines on a prickly pear cactus. These words make people uneasy. "Today's workplace is about taking risks!" they say, "It's not the job of businesses or organizations to make it safe for people. It was playing it safe that got us into problems in the first place."

Creating *safe space* is not about taking care of people at the expense of disallowing them the responsibility for taking care of themselves. Rather it's about creating balance: empathy and expression, flexibility and clear expectations, individualized approaches and accountability for results, people as human beings and people as producers of goods and services, open-endedness and boundaries. Safe space is about creating workplace context, containers where people are more likely to show up in their wholeness than in their need to protect old hurts from childhood.

Safe space is also about *allowing,* or at least, *not blocking,* not protecting and fortifying all the perimeters from the creeping reality of chaos. It is embracing chaos, becoming fluid and changing. To use a metaphorical example, to move from being nouns to being verbs.

At both a metaphorical and a reality level, *safe space* is about incorporating circles, open-ended processes that don't necessarily require an immediate solution, about creating shared meaning in work groups, bringing the *feminine essence* into the world of work. I'm not talking about replacing the hard-driving, task-oriented, bottom line approach; I'm talking about bringing balance into that approach with processes that are more about *allowing* than fixing, *creating dialogue* rather driving home one fixed point of view, *finding shared meaning* rather than imposed meaning, *inviting people to show up* rather than legislating them to perform. I deeply believe that this balance is our only option for survival, both personally and within the world in which we live and work. This is safe space. This is Open Space.

For further information:
Suzanne Maxwell
PO Box 973/11 Atole Way
Placitas, New Mexico 87043
USA
Telephone 505-86 7-3942